Published by
CSB Innovations, Dublin, TX 76446
Copyright© 2023 K. K. Smith

ISBN: 9781952330575

Obscure

To Anyone,
"You *are* worthy of your dreams. Just take the damn rock and run with it."

--yourself <3

PART ONE

LOCATION: E-MATE BASE, SINITALLIOUS

SEASON: LATE SUMMER

YEAR: 2203

001

PROMOTION

[ERIC]

[They] said an Anchor is someone who masks or focuses another person's powers. They even go on to say that manipulation is a common thread that [he] used. It's not a surprise but if I ever meet the guy, he'll get a piece of my mind.

From "My Thoughts"--SRP

The email ordered me back to his office at the end of the day. I'd already talked to him this morning about my situation with paying the bills at home, so he told me he'd figure something out for me. Not an hour later did he order me back to his office after my shift.

That was three minutes ago.

I twist a fringe in my pocket as I lean on the opposite wall to the door. I pause to think.

I'd managed to get patrols done before lunch. I even got some time in to write Sonia another letter--it's been hard to write when there's nothing else to say other than "I pray for your health today and every day after. Yours, Eric." I've been meaning to put in some hours so that I can go and visit her. I trust the Garner's are taking good care of her, but I just have this feeling. This feeling . . . I can't stay away from her like I did mom.

Not again.

"Your turn," a voice chimes. Kane. His sign for stepping out of Valmore's office was, "Good luck in there."

I don't see why everyone likes him. "Yeah, thanks, man."

"I'll see you later."

I hope not.

I let the door shut behind me, and I sit in front of Valmore's desk. He hands me a file. "What's this?"

"Open it and find out."

I do as he says. The promotion confirmational slip is on the top. "Does this mean I'll be getting more money?"

"Almost."

I almost let the papers slip from my hands. Expectations were growing more and more time-consuming. *When will I ever get back to you, Sonia?*

"You've got a new job. That's all. If you do it right, then

your pay will be increased every Friday." He nods to the papers under the slip and I move it away to gape at the picture at the top left corner.

"You can't be serious."

There she was. The girl.

"Deathly so."

Now I could put the name to her face. *Wanda Cannon.* Pretty.

"Only our best men can be around her. She's not to be underestimated just because she's a girl."

How could anyone underestimate her? Everyone on base drooled over her when Petition day came up. It was the only holiday for everyone that we had off from patrols and work. And it'd been the best interest of the Meds to allow those who'd wanted to see her, see her. She was a display really. The Meds had scheduled her final treatment and no one hesitated to go watch the Meds poke and prod at her for an hour.

I was there like everyone else. Except, while everyone was whispering about her body and her fine skin or whatever perves talk about, I was thinking about my poor little sister. That's what would happen to her if I forced her into a coma. If I made the decision to slow her death risk by putting her under years at a time.

Why is there no cure yet for the Marked?

"What's the job?"

"You've been assigned to Ms. Cannon as a Guide."

"A Guide?" I flipped loosely through the rest of the pages of her file. "What's that supposed to entail? You can't seriously tell me it means I'm babysitting her, can you?"

"No. Your job is to watch her closely. Observe her actions and decisions for analysis--,"

"So, babysitting then." I roll my eyes. "How is this a promotion?"

"This is a job given by the King himself. Only a select few are allowed this opportunity. Do you not think you're up for the job?"

I shook my head.

I was thinking back to Petition day. After everyone filed out, I lingered in the back for only a couple more minutes.

"She's beautiful isn't she?"

I stood sharp and stiffened my shoulders. "You could say that."

"Did you enjoy the show?"

I wouldn't call it that. "It's not my kind of scene."

I turned my head to the figure moving up beside me. Everything but his eyes were black. His gaze faced mine and he pondered, "Then why have you stayed longer than anyone else?"

Because I feel as though I understand her more than anyone knows.

My eyes closed for a moment to clear the memory. My focus was on Valmore again. "No. I can handle any job you give me. I just need to know if I'll be compensated for the extra work I'll be putting in for you *and* the King."

"When the job is done right, money won't have to be your concern anymore, Florbal. You can bet your life on that."

The sooner I can get this done, the sooner I can see Sonia again.

"When do I start?"

"One week from today. The night of the Meilo Dinner Party. She will need to be escorted there and back without incident."

I stood for the door. "Seems easy enough."

He shook his head with an airy laugh. "Don't underestimate her, soldier. She is a very weak individual."

"If she's weak, won't she follow orders easier than most?"

He shook his head again. "Let me finish. She is a weak individual indeed. But not only is she weak, but she's unstable. Not only to herself but to those she encounters. That includes you. She takes any opportunity to get under your skin so she can get what she wants. And I'm sure she will play the sympathy card on you the moment she's alone with you. Don't give in."

Maybe if I get to understanding her, she might be the key to saving Sonia . . .

I pull the frame ajar and give a stern nod. "You can count on me, sir. There's no job I can't handle."

002

OLD GRANTS

[CALLIE]

Dean gripped my hand tightly.

I whispered, "When do you think we'll get there?"

"I don't know."

Both of us knew where we were going. It was obvious because when the soldiers in navy blue uniforms shoved us into the vehicle, one spoke of General Underwood being pleased with finding us so quickly.

General Underwood. That was my father's title when he worked on base. But when he and my mother died, that title went to his younger brother, Shawn. My uncle.

I was really young when my parents died. So was Dean. Both of us lost our parents around the same time. But Dean was luckier than I was when he lost them. He didn't have anyone left in his family and that made him an orphan living in the streets. He was living my dream because I, on the other hand, was stuck with my uncle. Since he's the only living relative in my family, I didn't get to choose a better place to stay. He moved into my house before I knew it, and for a long time, I felt trapped.

Dean leaned in and whispered, "I don't like this feeling, Cal."

"Neither do I."

We weren't looking forward to seeing my uncle again. It's been a while since we'd seen him. A couple of years ago, he had his men take us to meet him on base, and he didn't show. It's as if he was going to play us again.

"Hey, look." I peeked out the window to where Dean was pointing. We were driving past the old hospital. "I bet Wanda's hating it in there."

Wanda. Our closest friend. We had been so close when we were younger; I can't remember the last time we saw her. I think it was in fourth grade.

"She's all alone in there without us."

I nodded my head. Both of us missed her. More than anything in the world. When Wanda was carried away in an ambulance, both of us hoped she'd make it through her sickness. We didn't expect the call from her parents when they found out their only child had died.

"I don't think she's alone anymore, Dean."

He shook his head. Out of the both of us, he still held onto the hope that Wanda didn't really die. Even after seven years, he still believes these crazy conspiracies about her; like the one about the doctors holding her in a lab so they could do tests and experiments on her. He told me that the Meds were keeping her in a secret section of the hospital so they wouldn't be disturbed.

I don't really believe what he says about her, but I don't shut him down. A little piece of me holds on just as much as he does. But I know she's dead. I was at her funeral where her parents wept over her closed casket. Though I thought it was strange that they would want one, at the time, I didn't think twice about it.

One of the soldiers' walkies came to life with some bad interference. "TSH—Check, fifteen minutes out, over. TSH—Check, fifteen minutes out, TSH, over."

The soldier held his walkie to his mouth. "Clear check, over. Clear check. Over out."

Dean's hand tightened around mine.

Almost there.

Dean cleared his throat. "Can one of you two tell me why Underwood didn't just come and visit us like a normal person?"

The soldier who spoke in the walkie shifted his shoulders. "General Underwood doesn't have time for visits."

"Then why does he want to visit with us? You're not really helping him out here."

The soldier took a long pause to stare between the two of us. "General Underwood stated that it's imperative you cooperate with us. No action is needed."

"No action is needed? You tell that jack—!"

"Dean! Stop."

He curled his fist with irritation. "Callie, this isn't right! Your uncle doesn't have the right to just barge into our lives and start asking things of us without getting what he deserves."

"I know you don't like this Dean, neither do I, but we need to see him before we can start bringing him down a peg. Definitely more than one of course."

"Like he would show his face to us. He didn't even show up the last time he pulled this stunt."

"That was three years ago. He's not a great person, I know, but he was probably busy. Ease up."

"Why are you giving him your sympathy? He's not just a

terrible person, but an even worse uncle. Have you forgotten what he's done? To you? To me?"

My anger was rising. "How could I forget? Every day I'm grateful I don't live under the same roof as him anymore!" I pulled my hand out of his and crossed my arms. "Why are you mad at *me*?!"

"I'm not mad at you! I'm mad at him! How could I ever forgive him?"

He still held a grudge over him from when we were little. It was only a few months before Wanda would be taken away, and Uncle Shawn was packing the last things for his trip. He told me he'd be back in a couple weeks.

"Why can't he stay, uncle? He doesn't have anywhere to go!"

"No boys are going to be sleeping in the same house as my niece. End of discussion."

"I can't live here alone! I need him!" I had started pulling at his suit jacket sleeve.

"You don't need anyone to depend on. Now, leave it!"

"But uncle—!"

"I said END OF DISCUSSION!"

He tried to pull his sleeve free, but I didn't let up so easily. "Please uncle! He won't do anything bad!"

The sound of the front door closing stiffened my stance. I told Dean to wait for my uncle to leave before coming in, but I guess he had heard us yelling. My uncle shoved me aside, and with a loud rip of fabric, Uncle Shawn's nice suit jacket was ruined. He didn't notice it until my body slammed into the floor, my head pounding from the harsh impact.

He was at my side in a second, pulling me up only to slap me across the face once, twice, three, or four times, I couldn't count with my head spinning. His voice had rung through my ears. "I paid good money for this suit and you ruined it! You useless piece of—!"

The last couple of scenes are fuzzy. I can't remember much, and the only thing that stuck was the sight of Dean cradling me close, his face freshly beaten and bruised, his nose bleeding. The sounds of a car peeling off had been in the distance.

I tighten my jaw and look into Dean's brown eyes.

At the time, I had no clue that what Uncle Shawn was doing to me for so long was bad. For so long I would just stand there and take it because I believed I deserved it for being a bad niece. But knowing now that he was only abusing me, I had nothing to show that I was at fault for anything.

I'm still grateful for what he did that day. Who knows what my uncle would've done to me if Dean hadn't come in to stop him. It made me think about Dean's theory about Wanda being alone.

I shift in my seat so I can rest my head on his shoulder. My only hope is that he'll forgive my anger toward him. "I really do miss her, ya know."

In a moment, I felt the warm touch of is his kiss on my head. I could feel him smiling as he spoke, "We'll get her back. Promise."

003

OLD PAIN

[CALLIE]

I was growing restless. We'd been waiting in my uncle's office for an hour. It really wasn't long to wait, but when it came to my uncle there was no saying he'd even show up. So, I wasn't going to wait any longer. I stood ready to leave, Dean right behind me.

The soldier guarding the door stuck out his hand to stop us. "Sit down."

"We're leaving," I say. "It's obvious that my uncle isn't coming. So, let us by."

He shook his head. "You can't leave. Just sit down and wait a little longer."

I stuck my finger in his chest. "Then you should take our place and tell my uncle when he comes in that we left."

I shifted to move around him, but he blocked my path. "Sit down. I won't ask again."

I let out a sarcastic laugh. "And what are you gonna do if we don't?" I looked at his nametag pinned to his breast pocket. "Look here, Brooks. I know you're doing your job. Just don't for a minute. Okay? If you don't let us pass, you won't like me very much."

He flooded my space with his cologne. "Sit down."

Dean pulled at the back of my shirt. He knew what was coming. "Listen, man, I wouldn't test her if I were you. Just let us pass."

He didn't listen. "Sit do--"

BAMM! My fist hit his face square in the nose. He reared back in surprise and when he clutched at his face, he left himself wide open for me to knee him in the groin. He collapsed within a second, and I stepped over him.

I waved Dean over to follow. "Come on, let's go!"

He was snickering down at the soldier. "I told you."

"Dean." he looked up and nodded. He followed close behind me as we sped down the halls. I knew where I was going so the only thing to slow us down was the chance of running into more soldiers. I kept a watchful eye on every crossing hall but didn't see the girl walking with a stack of papers until I was colliding with her. Her papers flew--some files emptied of their contents--and scattered all over the floor.

"I-I'm so sorry! I should have been watching where I was going--"

"No, no! It's my fault." She was trying to clean up the mess. "Here, let us help." Dean and I leaned down to gather papers fast. Even though we caused the girl to lose her papers, we didn't want to be sitting ducks.

I took my stack of papers and shoved them in the girl's view. She took them with a smile and I caught a glimpse at the files she had in her hands. Within a moment I had grabbed Dean's stack and shoved the papers in the girl's hands. I didn't waste time dashing us around the corner and down more halls.

"What's wrong, Cal?"

I don't speak till we're in the front foyer of the building. Dean's pulling me away from the doors to our freedom. His eyes are of concern.

"Those files," I rasp out. "They had our names on them. All three of ours?"

"What do you mean? All three. . . ?"

I take a large intake of air and release it. "Wanda. You, me, and Wanda."

His face turned dark in a split moment of grief and happiness. I knew what he was thinking before he even said it. *How could she be here?*

"But how? Is it. . . an old file? Surely,"

I shook my head. "I didn't want to look any longer. I just want us to get out of here." I tried pulling us toward the doors but he held me back. "Dean, we can't stay here!"

He let go of my hand. "You mean, you can't stay here. I can. I can get Wanda out of here. I know my way around. I'm sure if I--,"

I started to hear the pounding feet of men coming our way. My heart was picking up pace. I didn't want to be here.

But I couldn't leave without Dean. "Please," I pleaded, "We have to go."

He shook his head. "We can't leave Wanda here."

The footsteps were growing louder. My anger was rising. "Dean. She's not here."

"You said it yourself she was!"

"She's dead, Dean! You need to let her go!"

"No!"

"Yes! She's dead. She's been dead for seven years now! Why won't you accept that?!"

I felt my feet becoming antsy to move. To *run*! I needed to grab Dean and run and never look back. But, I forced myself to become a brick wall. Unable to move. I wasn't going to leave without Dean by my side.

"Why can't you accept that she never did! I know she's alive!"

"How! Your *magical* connection to her?" I say sarcastically. My jealousy was bubbling up.

This is not the time, nor the place.

"There's a connection, yes!"

UGH! "Then you should have stayed by *her* side! Then, you wouldn't be wasting my time here with your sad ass hopes of her still being alive!"

"How could you not believe? She's your friend!"

"Was! She *was* my friend until the day she died of an illness no one can cure yet!" His face turned solemn. I couldn't help but break under it. I sighed. "Dean, you know as well as I do that both of us loved her unconditionally. But, she died. There's nothing to bring those who have died back. That file must be an old one. She couldn't have lasted that long with how sick and frail she was."

Dean was searching my eyes. He never wanted to give up on Wanda. Not ever. I knew it was hard for him to hear.

His voice was low and deathly quiet. With the room slowly filling with men, I was the only one to hear him say, "Then why would they have a file on her if she wasn't alive? Huh? Answer that."

I shuddered, not straying my eyes from his. All I could do was swallow the growing lump in my throat. I didn't know what to say.

"Callie. Look how much you've grown!"

Dread filled me. I turned to see Uncle Shawn. He's in uniform, posture perfect, and his grin wicked. I put on a plastic smile for him when I speak, "What a surprise to see you again, uncle!"

I was watching his men--I count eight--as they crept around in a circle to incase us. We were trapped.

"Leaving so soon?" My uncle says.

"Not anymore," Dean growls.

"Why bring us here, uncle? Why not stop by instead?"

He shifts forward slowly. I hold my ground. "You sound upset to see me, dear," he coos mockingly. "I thought you'd want to see me since--,"

"Since what?" I felt Dean wrap his hand around mine. *Wanda.* He squeezes it.

I catch uncle staring at our entwined hands before his smile returns with a vengeance. "Since I assume you've heard about the miracle roaming around the halls."

I wanted him to say it out loud. "Whatever do you mean?"

"You know who I'm talking about, dear."

I shake my head, trying not to give myself away. Dean can feel my stiffness I know. He shifts himself in front of me.

"Your friend, Ms. Wanda Cannon. Surely you haven't forgotten her already."

"She's been dead for seven years, uncle."

His men move in closer. I push Dean forward to put space between us. I have a bad feeling this may turn ugly in a few minutes.

"It was all a cover-up."

I feel Dean stiffen. "Don't toy with us old man."

Uncle Shawn turns his attention to him. His only emotion. . . pure anger laced with irritation. "It's a small lie to protect secrets. You of all people should know that."

What was he talking about? "I can't believe what's not in front of me."

His eyes were on me again. "I've invited you to dinner tonight. That's where you'll be able to see her for yourself. Though, if you don't want to see her, you can stay in my office to sulk. Either way, neither of you are allowed to leave."

"And why not?"

"Because. I'm your guardian, and you aren't allowed to disobey my orders."

"You don't own me."

I could tell that his irritation was growing. His patience thinning. "Until you turn eighteen, you are under my protection. You follow my rules or I have my men drag you by your hair. Your choice."

I felt Dean shifting his body to shield me. I could feel my insides twisting into knots. I didn't want to fight, but if I needed to, I won't hesitate to protect what I know is right. I have my own rights. No one can change them. Not even my uncle.

"Why do you want me in your life now? You never wanted me around when I was younger. What changed?"

"I'd been getting reports that you'd been in one too many underground arena fights."

"You've been spying on me?"

He shook his head. "Call it what you want, but I have my ways. Plus it's an opportunity to spend time with you. Don't you think?"

Lies. "What do you really want from me?"

He moved forward. I fisted my hands, ready for anything. He said, "It's not what *I* want, but what someone wants from you. If you stay for dinner, then you may understand what I mean."

I move my body up against Dean's. My arms wrap around his arm tightly. He pulls me away as Uncle Shawn tries to caress my face. "You lay one hand on her again, and it's not just going to be my anger handed to you."

It's a threat I know churns malice in my uncle's heart. If Dean fights my battles, I fight his. No one messes with one expecting the other not to respond with repercussions. If Wanda was here, I'd fight her battles. Both of us would. She'd fight for us too, that I know.

I didn't want to believe my uncle's words about her being alive, but seeing is believing, right? Once I see that she's not at dinner I'll know I was right. Though a small piece of me aches for her to be alive, I know if I hope even a little, I'll crack under the pressure. I'll shatter into a million pieces *again*. I can't handle it. I don't want to handle it.

Not to mention, he'd hold the fights over my head as blackmail. It's illegal in our city. And with things getting harder with rebels rioting all around, I'd be facing some real jail time. Time I couldn't lose.

"I guess I'll see to believe tonight, uncle."

His wrinkled face cracked into a vicious grin. "Yes, you will."

004

IT'S NOT AN INVITE

[WANDA]

I can't say I was happy to see Valmore when I rolled over half-asleep. With one glance, my nerves sprung to life and I was jumping up to put distance between us.

"It seems you're feeling better. Did sleep help?"

I was shaking my head. "Sure."

Last night we were in the library talking over politics. I wasn't really paying attention to his lecture, since technically it wasn't something of importance to me. But when this sudden wave of nausea swam over me, it seemed a mist washed over my vision. I had blacked out only to come back collapsed on the floor in his arms, the sound of birds chirping around the room. I could have sworn that the room switched from a thick forest filled with greenery to balding browns and neutrals.

"Do you hear that?" I had asked.

His clear confusion was answer enough when he

responded with, "No? Are you feeling okay?"

I had shaken my head. Not even remotely. I felt completely drained physically and mentally. With that, he scooped me up in his arms and we were off to my hospital room.

I can't remember anything further. Did he stay here all night?

"So, did sleep help?" He asked again.

I cleared my thoughts with a slight shake of my head. "Yeah, I'm alright." I couldn't look into his eyes. "You didn't have to stay."

"I thought you would want someone to be here if you woke up." he stood from his chair, "Plus, I wasn't here the whole time. I spoke to the Meds about what happened," I felt there was something bad about to be said, "and you'll be starting to take your medication twice a day. Two in the morning and two before you go to bed."

I could live with that.

A couple of months ago the Meds told me I had to take this medication. At first, I didn't mind, but after a couple of weeks, I could feel my whole body growing weaker. It was as if I was ten again, becoming mysteriously ill. So, when the Meds would drop off my medication in the morning, I would pretend to pop it into my mouth and swallow. When they left, I would stuff the pills into a sock until I could dispose of them in my growing stash in my hiding spot.

Looks like I'm going to have to make more trips to the courtyard than I had thought. *I need to remember to move my hiddy-hole before someone accidentally stumbles upon it.*

I was aware of Valmore's growing stare. "What?" I bite out. "Did you stay because you're here to take me to my next task?" I wanted to rip his head off with my words. *Why can't he just leave me alone for once?*

He seemed to not acknowledge my disdain for him. That, or he didn't care. "You'll be training in combat for the next couple of months."

I couldn't hold back my shock. "Are you serious?! You're really going to let me train in combat!"

He held up his hand to stop me. "I wasn't the one to make the call. I only make sure I enforce it."

I almost didn't care. "Do I start today? Is that why you've been waiting?"

"Yes and no. I came back so I could tell you about the dinner party tonight." I wanted to cut in but he held up his hand again. "You must attend. No exceptions."

"But—,"

"I know, I know! I'm not going to let you go in that." He gestured to my sweatpants and a baggy shirt. "I went ahead and got," he pulled out a box from under his chair. *Why hadn't I noticed that until now?* "This."

I didn't move to open it. I didn't want to.

"I think you'll really enjoy coming. I was told that some of your friends will be there as well."

Wait . . . *Oh, my word!* "Callie and Dean."

He was a villain, nodding his head methodically slow.

I shifted forward. He has to be lying. Callie and Dean couldn't have come. Not because of me. Not because they remembered me. It's been too long!

I rasped out, "They can't be here."

"Oh, yes they can, dear. He wanted them here as well."

"Who?"

He was at the door disregarding my question, "I've assigned a guide to you. He'll be by to pick you up at six o'clock. Don't be late, dear. It reflects badly on me."

The door shuts and I'm left looking at the box wrapped with a pretty red bow.

I released the tight breath I'd been holding. *How was I supposed to handle this? Were my friends really here? For me?*

I drag my feet as I walk slowly back to my room. I'm gripping my empty sock firmly in my grasp, twisting it clockwise, and then when I can't twist any tighter, unraveling it and twisting counter-clockwise. I successfully dumped the pills I had been stuffing in my sock and stashed them into my hiddy-hole in the courtyard. It's a small thing, really. Only ten by ten feet, dead grass and a flower pot laid upside down in the corner. I'm the only one who knows about it.

I stop in my tracks. A tall soldier stands at my door. *Is that my guide? Is it time already?* I glance at the clock down the hall. Six o'clock. He spots me and turns. I clear my throat and dash for my door. He makes space for me to pass and I shut it on him. "Sorry!" I shout. "Don't come in, I'll be out in a minute!"

I dumped my clothes on the floor by the foot of my bed and grabbed the red bow. Untying it and pulling the lid to the side, I let out a short gasp. Valmore remembered.

I pull the lavender-colored silk dress out and rush to pull it over my head. It fit perfectly. Its spaghetti straps comfortably on my shoulders and the tight corset middle hugging my body, making me feel like I'm being held by the sun—as if arms were around me to keep me safe from the bitter bite of the breeze. The skirt falls to the floor, hiding my feet that I shoved in the low heels that matched the dress.

What about my hair?

I flip it and twist the wavy curls into a low bun. Now I'm ready.

I close the door behind me. "Shall we go?" I look up at the soldier only for a moment. It's all I need to be captured by his piercing green eyes. They captivate me. They hold me in a snare I can't find a way out of. I clear my throat. I feel my face fill with color. "I don't think we've properly introduced ourselves." I stick out my hand. "I'm Wanda Cannon."

He looks at my hand and doesn't take it. His eyes sharpen my breath as he speaks. "Florbal. Your guide."

"Right." I was so distracted by his eyes that I forgot Valmore sent him. I tighten my jaw. "My personal guard. Shall we go then?" I say.

There's only a slight nod of his head and we're off.

005

NOT WHAT I THOUGHT

[WANDA]

Climbing up the familiar stairs to the top of the Grand Hall, my guide--Florbal--pushes open the double doors. When I thought we would meet silence inside, I was greeted by chaos. Dozens upon dozens of soldiers stood around in their best uniforms--all blacks and blues, the colors of E-MATE I've noticed--chatting and laughing with each other. Most of the men turned to look at me, some of their eyes--I noticed-- gazing me up and down like a midnight snack. My discomfort was eminent when I also noticed them looking at my guide over my shoulder, jealousy lacing their expressions. I felt as if my exposed skin was too much to show, giving fuel to the fire that had been lit by Valmore's constant presence. I wanted to crawl out of my skin.

Florbal's hand was at my lower back, pushing me through the crowd to the dining hall. It seemed we both had the same thought of discomfort.

I hadn't realized how big the front foyer was.

I look back at the library. It stands across from the dining hall.

"Don't forget to smile."

I try to make space between us as we come closer to the doors. "Why do I need to smile for anyone?"

There's a slight twitch to the edge of his lips and I almost want to call it a hidden laugh. His clear-cut voice ruined the thought immediately. "Just, don't forget to smile."

In front of the doors, he has me pause. Someone was announcing my presents inside. The doors started to open slowly as if time was slowing down just for me.

I stepped in and tried to forget that Florbal was still on my heels, breathing down my neck. From what I remember him telling me moments ago, I placed a smile across my face. One that I try to mask with irritation. I didn't want a single soul in this room to think I wanted to be here.

I felt his hand on my arm. I didn't pull back. Everyone was staring at me for a moment. I didn't like all their eyes. Someone proclaimed, "Thank you for coming, Ms. Cannon! Please, take your seat."

Florbal is gently pulling me to my spot. It's on the left side by the open windows and square in the middle of the table.

He sits next to me and I'm relieved because he's the only face that's familiar. I could still feel everyone's eyes on me and I felt uncomfortable. I couldn't dare to look around to see if I knew anyone else.

I never liked being the center of attention. I just wished I was no one.

I bowed my head to hide my eyes. The announcer who welcomed me only a minute ago raised his voice in a gleeful proclamation of excitement. "And finally! The one person you've all been waiting for is here! Please rise in honor of his majesty--!" I reluctantly stood like everyone else, hesitant to look at anyone in particular. No one's eyes were on me anymore. Their gaze was on the doors I had come through just moments ago.

My intrigue peaked. Could it be a king? I've never seen one before. I leaned over the table so I could see who everyone was looking at. In the books, I read about royals who dressed in fancy-colored silks and robes that enveloped them. Men would have fluffy beards and long locks that were silk-smooth around their shoulders. Gold rings covered their hands and gem-covered necklaces and crowns would shine on them.

I had my hands on my guide's back so I could hold my view.

The doors slowly pulled back. I couldn't spot him through all the people standing in front of the table. I was secretly happy that Florbal was here. I leaned in enough that he had to be holding me up. "Your Majesty, King Peter the Second!"

Everyone around the room shifted to salute him and the man waved at them. "Please!" He laughed, his voice a force that could shake the room. "There is no need for such formalities here! Please, everyone, sit."

Don't be scared.

I froze. *Who's there?* I look around the room. Was someone trying to get my attention? No one seemed to look my way, that I could see. Florbal shifts and I'm pulled back out of my thoughts. I sit when he does. Everyone is in conversation about who just arrived. I'm not the only one who squirms in my seat with both unease and excitement.

"Can you believe it?"

"--I feel so lucky!"

". . . I can't believe he actually came--,"

"--didn't think he would!"

I watch as the man--King Peter--moves gracefully to his seat. He's a monster of a man. A King, but he didn't look at all like one. I catch a familiar face, but I'm too fixated on who King Peter is. How he looks.

Servers place plates of food in front of us while I scope out the final guest. His suit is all black, no color other than the silver watch on his right wrist. His hair is cleanly cut close on the sides and gelled forward but as to not bag over his forehead and into his eyes. His skin is olive and dark for a king who sits around all day. It denies all assumptions, that he actually gets out a lot more than I would expect. Though I'm too far to read his eyes, their dark and menacing glare is answer enough to not delve any further. Could he be the one who spoke in my head? Surely that's not possible. *But it sounded so familiar . . .*

I grab my fork and stab at a small potato before glancing at my guide. He's staring at me. "What?"

He shakes his head. "Nothing," he drops his voice for only me to hear, "sorry. You just . . . reminded me of someone." he turned back to eating the meat on his plate.

I felt someone's eye at the back of my head so I turn and caught a familiar gaze. I couldn't quite put my finger on who it was but I turned away before I wanted to know. I didn't exactly like the gut-clenching feeling I got from seeing him.

"Who'd I remind you of?"

"Huh?" Florbal turned. "Oh, it's no one." he looked at my plate and back again. "You might as well eat. Don't want it to get cold."

I felt he was dodging my jab at him. I held his gaze for

a moment longer, then turned to eat the baby potato I had stabbed with my fork. My mouth filled with saliva as I hummed quietly with satisfaction. I smiled as I popped another one into my mouth.

This is really good, I whispered to myself. *This is so deliciously good!*

006

Time rolled into two hours. In the first one, King Peter dined with everyone and conversed with most of the men and women at the end of the table. But when his plate was cleaned of its contents, he stood and apologized to the room. "I must be going. I'm saddened I can't stay any longer, but duty calls."

He left without another word. There was a pause when the doors closed behind him, but once the pause was over, everyone was back into their own conversations. I didn't listen to any of them or care to look at their faces. I rather stared between them and passed time counting the minutes between taking a sip of my water or a bite of my food. When the time neared the end of the second hour, people started to clear their plates and leave.

A small group that sat by me stood to leave after a couple of minutes. I stand after them and Florbal grabs my arm. "Where are you going?"

I pulled myself free when he stands. "I need to go to the

restroom." I step back to make space between us. "Can I not go anywhere by myself?" I turn to leave. He's right behind me. *I guess not.*

When I reached the door to the girl's bathroom I turned sharply on him. "So help me, if you come in here with me, I'll knock you into next week." I pushed the door in and watched it close in his face.

He's not gonna come in. Good.

I step into the first stall and take a deep breath. I can finally breathe again.

When I was sitting in that room, I felt trapped. Not only did I hate everyone's occasional eyes on me when they were in conversation but, the face that they made when I did catch a glimpse of them before they would turn away was enough for me.

A surge of emotions came over me. All at once, I was back to the first day of school when I had no friends to talk to. Everyone looking my way and laughing before turning to whisper something to their friends. *I want to cry.*

I feel so alone all in one moment and I squeeze my eyes shut trying to think of anything else. Once my heart slows and my hands stop shaking I stand and flush my business away. I wash my hands and take one last moment of privacy before opening the door and stepping out.

I couldn't see my guide anywhere. *Where is he?*

"Don't you look beautiful, dear!" My head snaps to Valmore's voice. He's walking toward me with his arms out to give me a hug. *Did he send Florbal away?* I take a side step to avoid him.

"Nice to see you too, Valmore." I cringe. "I see you're dressed up too."

"Yes indeed, dear. Did you enjoy dinner?"

Always straight to interrogation with you. "Yeah." I give a smile. "I especially liked the baby potatoes they served." I try to put on a counter before he questions me more. "I didn't see you. Were you in the dining hall as well?"

His eyes twitched slightly. "Yes. I can't blame you if you didn't spot me. There were a lot of fresh new faces around."

We didn't say anything for a long moment before I jabbed, "Am I allowed to leave now? I've had enough dress-up to last a lifetime."

He shook his head. "Not yet, dear." I took his outstretched arm hesitantly as he led me back to the dining hall. "Someone wants to meet with you."

"Who?"

Two soldiers opened the doors for us. Not a second after I released Valmore's arm am I being rammed into by a body. Being spun in a circle.

"You're okay!"

"It really is you." another chimes.

I look at the voice. Callie stands only a couple of feet away, her feet frozen mid-step. Callie, my friend who doesn't look any different from when we were younger. Her caramel waves float on her shoulder. Her blue eyes screaming her emotions without her even trying. In a moment my heart drops to the floor and I glance down at the figure holding me in his tight embrace.

"Dean-!" I look to the side again. I'm being rammed by another body—Callie's as I can see. "Callie! You guys are really here!"

My heart came to life, racing at a speed I would never catch. It was full and they were warm, their tight hug enough to bring the biggest smile to my face. My cheeks started to hurt with the unused muscles.

This all seemed like a dream.

"You guys are really here!" I repeated. "You didn't forget me after all!"

Dean set me on my feet and held his arms out holding my shoulders. "We never forgot about you, Wanda."

Callie caresses the side of my face. I lean into her warmth, my body aching for her touch. "We missed you so much!" Dean's hands dropped for Callie to pull me into a tight embrace. I squeeze her closer to me and she follows the same.

I hear her sniffle and she pulls back enough to face me. "I thought I'd never see you again. You have no idea how much I've missed you!"

Dean's arms wrapped around us and we both turned to laugh at him. The faint memory of being held in their arms like this came to view. We were so little when we all became friends. It felt so far away in a moment.

"Don't cry. You'll make *me* cry." Callie sniffled.

I blinked my tears away. "You're the one who's crying!" I laughed.

My chest filled. Like magic, I felt whole. Like somehow this, this right here, was the thing I needed to fill the growing void in my heart. I'd been so empty. No thoughts ever filled me more than now. Seeing them, here!

"You look so healthy." Dean cracks. "You don't look sick at all."

I smile at him. Shake my head. "Not anymore. I'm all better now."

"Not quite."

All of our heads turn. The familiar face from earlier. I step out of Callie and Dean's arms and stand in front of them. In front of . . . "You." I spit.

Callie pulled at my arm. "You always ruin these moments, uncle. Give us a minute at least."

Callie's only uncle. General Underwood. I remembered him well, now. I remembered the moments I wished I could bash his face in. So many times I wanted to kick him where it hurt because Callie had come to school with a black eye. He was always drunk from what she told me, and always yelling at her for doing something he didn't like.

I contemplate the idea of nailing him square in the jaw. I hold onto it as it is to ground me.

I had the faintest idea that he worked here. But he worked in commanding soldiers while Valmore had me studying. I had hoped it was a completely different General Underwood than the only one I knew at the time. *Apparently not.*

Dean was pulling me between him and Callie.

"You've had your fun," Callie growled. "Now she's coming with us and all of us are leaving."

General Underwood's face lifted into a wicked sneer. "You think you have authority here--how funny you are dear. Don't you remember what I said earlier?"

Callie stepped forward. She seemed to be holding her ground. *When did she finally start fighting back? I've never seen her like this--fierce.* "You never told me that she'd been here this whole time. She deserves to go home with Dean and I. Don't be getting in my way."

She was shaking. Either out of fear or the pure exhilaration of standing up to her uncle for once, I don't know. Probably both. I looked at General Underwood. *What was his move?*

I saw his jaw tighten and grow ridged. My blood ran cold in a moment and I reached for Callie's arm, trying to pull her back. The sudden urge to protect her from him was starting to boil.

He stepped into her space, making her fumble back. His voice was like the fierce bite of a blade. "Never, again, will you speak to me as if you have any power over me. I have all the means to take everything . . . *everyone*, away from you."

Closing the space between them when he spoke daggers through her heart made her shatter in a moment. She stepped back, her childhood terror clear on her face. As if he was cutting her skin with a serrated-edged sword, her body began to break down.

My heart even skipped a beat as he continued to speak, "I have *all* the power to take everything you have." He was practically spitting each word in her face. "I have every right to make you suffer without a shred of hope for a better tomorrow. I will make your life a living hell if you speak out of turn again. Am I understood?"

None of us moved. I could almost hear all of us swallow our throats out of fear of sudden movement. As if to satisfy his answer, he grabbed the front of Callie's collar and pulled her right into his face. She turned herself away, squeezing her eyes tightly shut.

"Am. I. Understood?"

Dean shifted closer, squeezing me tighter. Callie nodded her head roughly. "Yes . . . yes." She croaked. "You--you are understood, sir."

He dropped her. "Good." She stumbled back. Dean moved to catch her before she fell. I watched as she curled into Dean's chest, her shaking clear and definite. Something wasn't right. It almost feels as if he's holding something over them. It made my anger rage. I turned to General Underwood in a moment and he was smiling down at me.

"Sorry about that." He stuck his hand out for me to shake--as if nothing happened? And the same one that held Callie off her heels moments ago. "I've been so excited to meet you in person, for so long—" he hadn't seen it coming. He was stumbling backward, gripping his nose, "What the hell!?"

I could feel my fingers slowly growing numb. There was no holding back now. I didn't care what happened to me after this, but at this moment, all I wanted to do was make him pay for the abuse he laid upon his niece all these years. I dove at him and we fell to the ground. I pounded my fists into his face as hard as I could lay them. No one could stop me. Not even Dean, who I punched in the jaw at one point.

The satisfying crack of General Underwood's nose fueled the rage I had been bottling up for so many years. Not just for Callie, but for all the misfortune I had to go through just to feel like I never left my prison. I practically laughed as he screamed in agony. He was howling, and I was gritting my teeth. I threw as many punches down on him as I could.

Someone soon tackled me to the ground. My chest was short-winded as I tried to free myself from my guide's grasp. It was harsh and unmoving. "Let go of me! Let me go! "

I was throwing all the words I could at him. Slurs and curse words. "Let me at him! He deserves it, you son of a--! LET ME GO!" Florbal was getting me up and his arms were wrapped firmly around my waist, locking my arms to my side. I tried to free myself, but my chest was becoming tight.

"Hold her firm, soldier!" Underwood shouted. "Agh!" He gripped at his broken nose. Blood was dripping onto his suit as he heaved big breaths. "You B—augh! You little brat!"

I spit in his face. "GO TO HELL! YOU DESERVE IT—!"

"YOU BROKE MY NOSE!"

He let his nose go only to grab at my face. His blood-covered hand was gripping my jaw tight. I flinched, my chest still heaving. It was getting harder to breathe the more I fought.

"Don't hurt her!" I heard Callie choke.

Underwood's face was covered with bruises and two black eyes that were slowly becoming swollen. His left cheek was cut open and bleeding like his nose. "You broke my nose." He spat in my face. "You bitch." I tried to pull my head out of his grip but it only got tighter the more I struggled. "You'll pay for that."

He pushed at me and his hand left my face. I coughed out a weak laugh. I spit his blood at his feet. I took long, deep breaths.

"It seems you need more correcting than my niece, Ms. Cannon."

A soldier had his arms around Callie's middle as well. "Uncle, please,"

I grit my teeth. "Wouldn't *you* like to see that." Another deep inhale of air. "I'll kill you before then."

"Empty threats aren't going to scare me, little girl." He wipes at his nose and smears the blood. It still drips from his nostrils. Then he waves us away like pests. "Get her out of my sight, soldier. All of them!"

Florbal adjusts his arms around me and starts for the door. I look around the room. I don't see Valmore. Callie is gone first, Dean nowhere in sight. Her screams echoing away from me faster as we're right behind her.

I look back at Underwood one last time. A soldier is handing him a handkerchief to wipe his nose. "I'll kill you if you lay a hand on her again!" I shout. "Mark my words!"

"Empty threats, little girl." He looks back at me, a wicked smile full of blood on his face. "All you have Ms. Cannon is empty threats."

007

CRUEL SILENCE

[WANDA]

Once I was shut out of the Grand Hall, Florbal let me go. "Start walking."

I wanted to turn and give him cruel words but I held my tongue. He wasn't the one who really needed my untamed anger. I'll wait to give it to Valmore if he ever shows his face again.

Will he extend my trials? Will he make me sit in my room until General Underwood sees fit? Because all soldiers in combat report to him, right?

I don't want to think about the possibilities.

When we turn the corner to my hallway, heading to my room, I slow. Right in front of my door, a Med stands, holding something in her hand. She pushes her glasses up when she spots me. "Ms. Cannon, your medicine." She sticks out her hand. It's as if she already knows about the blood smeared all over my face.

I grab the paper cup and dump the pills in my palm. "Thank you." I nod at her before turning to my guide. "If your job is to watch me sleep, let me change before I let you in."

He didn't say anything. I looked back at the Med and popped the pills in my mouth. Sticking them under my tongue as I swallowed a large gulp of air was satisfaction enough for her and she left. I opened my door and closed it quickly. Spitting the pills into my hand, I rushed to stuff them into my sock. I take a tight breath before changing back into my sweats, using the end of the skirt to wipe off the dried blood still on my face. I let my hair fall around my shoulders as I chunk the dress and shoes into the trash.

I open the door and step to the side. Florbal stalks in and when I close the door, he's staring at me from his seat. It's the only one I have in my room and I normally find Valmore sitting in it most of the time. His eyes almost glow in the dim overhead lights. Curfew is at ten o'clock. I have the choice to turn my lights out early if need be but all lights go out at ten no matter what.

I look at the clock only for a moment before turning back. It's 9:55.

"What's your actual name?" I ask. "Because I don't think calling you Florbal is very cool."

There's a hint of gold that sparkled in his eyes as he narrowed them. *Is he contemplating on telling me?*

I roll my shoulders and sigh. "Look. I only want to know because I figured we'll be seeing each other more than we think. Valmore is always breathing down my neck. I think this is his way of doing that, without actually being here all the time." He doesn't move. "So, can you tell me? Please?"

Nothing. Then, his expression tightened. "How can you expect anything from me when you just pulled that stunt, tonight?"

I didn't want to answer.

"Fine." I sigh. "Have it your way," I whisper, walking to my bed and crawling under the covers. I roll so my back is toward him, closing my eyes. I didn't have to wait long before the lights went out and my mind drifted to other places. Sleep pulled me in and I drowned in its blackness.

008

NIGHT'S DEATH

[WANDA]

I shot up with a start. I grasped at my chest.

Another bad dream, I thought.

Looking around the room Florbal was still sitting in the chair. The position had grown closer to the corner and I assumed he'd done it while I was asleep. I couldn't help but stare at him as he slept so soundly.

It's calming, I think. Something I wish I could have.

Then I remember what I did last night. I remember Callie and Dean's faces. Underwood's bloody one. *It wasn't just a dream.*

The lights were out still, but the clock over the door glowed faintly in the dark.

3:24 a.m.

I sighed, throwing the blankets off of me. I stepped quietly toward the bathroom and closed the door before turning on the light. I turned the shower on and pulled a towel out of the small sink cabinets. I pull out fresh new clothes as well—a fitted black shirt with royal blue sweatpants.

Once I'm out, and I've brushed my teeth, I open the door. I wipe my hands on my sweats. Florbal is still sound asleep.

Good.

I slipped past things scattered around the floor, pulling up my dull shoes and tip-toeing past my sleeping guide. As I close the door behind me, I make sure to be extra quiet. Then I'm on my way to my secret hideaway.

"You do know that it's 5:00 in the morning, right?"

I'm startled by Florbal's voice as I turn away from the closing door to the courtyard. I hold my hand to my stomach, feeling it drop to my feet. "Yeah." I clear my throat. Shake the nerves. "I know," I look up at him. "How'd you find me?"

"I followed you." he yawns. I nearly drop my jaw. Instead, I tightened it out of fear. "Clearly, you don't know when someone is following you, even though there's no place to hide."

I bite the inside of my cheek. He had a point. Waving the worries aside, I try to move past him. He held his arm out to stop me.

"What?" I asked, "I can't go back to my room now?"

He shook his head. "Not until you tell me what's behind that door."

I felt as if my teeth were gonna break from the pressure. I release my jaw. "Why do you have to know?"

"Because it's my job to know. If you don't tell me, I'll just have to look inside myself. And clearly," his eyes prodded at my facial expression, "you don't want that to happen."

My head shook slightly. I didn't want to give up so easily, but his eyes just had to suck me in. "It's an abandoned courtyard."

"The hospital doesn't have a courtyard. You're lying."

I shook my head quicker. "No, really. This wing of the hospital has been under reconstruction for the last year. No one comes here."

"*You* come here. Why?"

I scrunch my brow. He didn't need to know everything.

But why did I feel the need to tell him so? "Valmore doesn't let me have my own space."

"So . . . you come here?"

I push at his arm and dip my head down. Walking a couple of steps in front of him, he grabs my arm, pulling me back. I look up at him again and dare tread his green waters, but then they falter and he lets go of my arm. *Is that sympathy I see?*

"Why do you hide here? Is it something to do with last night?"

"I don't--," thoughts flood me as I know fresh tears are welling up. Every day it seems home has grown farther and farther away from me. It feels as though my vision is growing dark. As if the possibility of getting back is growing thinner and thinner by the day. "I don't hide here," I sigh, "I breathe here."

009

UNDERSTANDING

[ERIC]

"*I breathe here*," is what she said before I let her walk away.

I breathe here.

What was that supposed to mean exactly?

I wanted to ask. Push farther for more information. But--her eyes. Those beautiful gray pools that speak emotions without any words. *Pretty isn't a word to describe her anymore.*

We were back in her room, my eyes never veering away from her form. She felt my gaze, I knew, and made it her mission to avoid my eyes at all cost. I was thankful because I wouldn't know what to do if I had the chance to gaze into those cold pools again, but how I wished for them to look deep into me. *What an absolute beauty they are.*

I think she fell back asleep again, her body still and calm. I let myself relax.

What am I doing? In less than twenty-four hours of actually meeting her in person, I've already developed a crush on her. *I mean, how could that be?* Could it be from reading her file? I knew everything about her, and yet when I first laid eyes on her all of that disappeared. There were little ques for her personality, but nothing as colorful as this. Not to mention, her file never spoke of the power she had within a punch. Man, could she throw one. It made me want to fall for her more.

I shook my head. I couldn't.

My eyes drifted closed after a while, and I didn't wake up until the rush of the door slamming into the wall startled me.

"GET UP YOU FOUL GIRL!"

I stood fast and moved in front of Valmore without a thought. Cannon was behind me, the bed between us. *She was startled just as much as I was.*

"HOW IDIOTIC CAN YOU BE? HOW STUPID CAN YOU GET?!" Valmore screamed. He didn't move, thankfully, but I put my arm out to block him if he did.

"Please listen, Val—"

"NO! You listen to me, Ms. Cannon!"

"Sir," I interjected.

"Get out of my face, soldier. Get out!"

"Sir—,"

"That's an order!"

I held my ground as he proceeded to push himself into my space. I was used to this by all my supervisors. This was no different. "Sir!" I pounded out. He fumbled over his growing irrational anger. He calmed as I did. "Please. Why don't we take this outside so we don't make a scene?"

His voice started to rise again toward Cannon. "It's too late--!"

I grabbed his shoulder. "Sir." I gave a slight tilt of my head, and he finally took my hint.

"Fine." He peered around me once more to jab at Cannon. "Don't move."

I left the door ajar, knowing--hoping--that Cannon would be listening in some capacity.

"I've gotta say, you really did a good job last night, soldier. You were quick on your feet and didn't hesitate to handle her."

"Thank you, sir--."

"I mean, how am I supposed to trial her if she has the chance to do that again? Underwood told me to take her out of training, but just last night King Peter told me my work was doing wonders. *Wonders!* What am I supposed to say to that; if he asks why she never did anything?"

"Sir,—"

"I mean, did you see her? What am I saying, of course, you did! She proved to be unstable and out of control." *I told you*, he's saying, "If she knew how to fight for real, who knows what she might do!"

"Sir, listen." I stopped him. "What do you plan to do? You can't seriously think about locking her up in here, now do you?"

I breathe here.

"It wouldn't be a bad idea."

"You can't do that." I counter back.

There was a pout coming from him. *He couldn't seriously be acting like a child.* "And why not?"

I couldn't just let this unfold. This was my job to save Sonia. But yet, Cannon could be the key to saving her rather than the money or the job itself.

In order to save one, I have to save the other.

I need to play my cards right. And that starts with not telling Valmore about Cannon's hideout yet. "You said it yourself. She's not only a danger to others but to herself. If you keep her caged up here, she'll become worse."

He actually looked to be thinking hard about this. He could have been speaking his next words to himself, "Then what am I supposed to do? Should I put her under again?"

"No," I responded, "That's not the way to go, sir."

"Then how am I--?"

"I believe she just needs to be trained."

He started to laugh as if I was joking. "Oh, you're serious!"

I nod.

"And who do you think would be up for the task? I don't think any man would want to tame a beast as wild as her."

He'd be surprised. Every man on base wishes to be in a room with her, alone. If you add training to that, who knows what'd they do.

"I'll do it," I say. He gives me a weird look. "I'll already be around her twenty-four/seven. Why not train her as well?"

"Are you really willing to put that on yourself? You said you were thinking about your--,"

"I can do it, sir," I cut in, "Seriously. Let me do this for you."

He gave a hesitant shake of his head. "I can't believe I'm doing this," he whispered under his breath, "Fine. I'll sort this out with Underwood."

I crack a smile and he pokes his finger in my chest.

"But! I'm putting you to the highest standards. Fail to complete them and I'm finding someone else. Got it?"

"Understood, sir."

He moves around me for the door. I move to block him for a brief moment. Once I hear Cannon's feet shift away from the frame I push it open for Valmore. He nods to me. I do the same as he enters.

"Today is your lucky day, Ms. Cannon." he projects onto her. "Dates have been moved, and your combat training will start at the beginning of next week. Florbal, here," both of their gazes move over me. I straighten as he continues. Cannon doesn't release my gaze. Did she get to hear everything? "--will be training you himself. So I expect great things. Hard work and no rough-housing. Last night was the one and only warning for you Ms. Cannon. Choose your next moves wisely."

Her gray pools move toward Valmore. "What about my friends? Callie? Dean?"

He avoided her question. "Your guide will accompany you everywhere you go. Unless I, or Underwood himself says otherwise, he stays." his gaze veers toward me. I re-adjust as he continues. "Curfew is at ten o'clock. No excuses."

I nod.

"I can set up arrangements so that you bunk in here with her so that--"

"Unnecessary." I quickly jab. I falter only a moment to look back at Cannon again. There aren't enough words to describe the fear I see in her eyes. The tightening of her chest at the words pooling from Valmore's throat like a leaky faucet. I turn back. "I'm perfectly fine. If I must sleep in a chair some nights, I will. There is no need for special treatment when the situation can be handled quite well without it. Thank you, but no thank you, sir."

He seemed to see something between the two of us. I know I wasn't giving anything up, but was I cracking? Was this girl, Wanda Cannon, gonna be my downfall?

Surely not.

He nodded. Satisfied.

"But what about my friends? I need to see them."

Valmore stopped halfway out the door. Turned back toward her and smiled. "I forbid you from seeing them. Underwood has enough to deal with them. Neither he nor I will allow you to see them until permitted by the King. Is that understood?"

Her jaw tightened.

"You can train. You can continue studying. But under no other circumstance are you allowed to leave this building without permission."

Her hands fist ghostly white while Valmore faces me. He whispers for only I can hear, "Keep a keen eye on her, soldier. I will be back to relieve you in a couple of hours."

I nod. Once he's gone, I close the door and face Cannon. She's slumped on the edge of the bed, her form shaking uncontrollably. I know she's crying, even though she's quiet. But I don't question it.

She's never left this place without someone right behind her. She's trapped in a place that saved her, and yet has never felt more held down by what she has. The only friends she's had in her life finally come back only to be thrown in her face and taken away because she had the nerve to stand up for them. No matter what step she takes, she's in the wrong, and no path for her can she swim back up to the surface for air.

I breathe here

I breathe here

I . . . breathe,

Here. "My name is Eric."

Her head turns slowly to face me. It's all puffy and pink from the restrained tears. "What?"

"My name," I clear my throat, "It's Eric."

In a moment her face softens with a smile. *So warm . . .*

"It's nice to meet you, Eric."

010

SPACED OUT

[WANDA]

Leaves whip around me

a tornado running over my body.

One moment I'm laying

on the soft ground,

Then,

I'm falling.

My breath leaves my lungs

I crash into the earth

A meteor with the weight of the world.

It's the fourth night I've woken up drenched in sweat, my heart racing a million miles a minute.

It's the night before my first day of training.

I get out of bed, knowing I won't be able to go back to sleep. After a long shower, I dress into my new uniform—a fitted royal blue shirt and a matched pair of cargo pants. I put my new boots on and dig out the key from my new hiding place—a small crack in the trim of the wall. I stuff it into my pocket and head down the halls. Once I'm inside the courtyard, I heave a ragged breath before sitting against the wall. I pull my knees close and lay my head against the wall, closing my eyes.

Eric will be here soon.

Eric. He hasn't stopped me from coming here. He hasn't questioned what's inside. He doesn't even open the door to peek.

Why?

He sits outside until I walk out. He'll knock to make sure I'm alright, but that's it. He treats me differently. Nicer.

I don't understand why.

"Should I put her under again?"

My stomach had collided with the floor. I thought my illness put me in my seven-year coma. Not Valmore himself. He told me that I'd been transferred to a hospital in Hightown before coming here. He told me my body forced me into a coma because my body and brain couldn't handle it all at once.

He told me the Meds saved me from dying in that state.

All lies.

Again.

I was standing.

The wind was blowing.

The trees' branches and

leaves billowing in the breeze.

It was peaceful.

Like pure bliss. Around,

There stood mountainous trees.

I smiled. I could feel

the breeze on my face, cold

Bittersweet. I was in a

dream

And yet it felt so real. I was lost

a sea of green all around.

I heard a rustle

in the bushes,

I spun around,

Shocked to see someone emerging;

from the green.

"Who are you?"

She looked as puzzled as me.

"Who are you?"

"I asked first!" she shouts.

She grabbed my hands

a surge of electricity swept

Both of us up. We gasped.

Energy burst through my body

Like a current.

Starting at my hands and up

up

up my shoulders,

through my torso, and finally

to my feet.

It exploded out

our bodies

out through the trees.

They moved with our energy instead of,

The wind around them.

It felt like we were the wind,

pushing at them all;

the trees around us, We were creating this!

A mass pulse of energy.

She stepped away;

quick breaths.

"What just happened?

Did you do that?"

I shook my head,

"No. I thought you were doing it.

What was it?!"

I stumbled forward

grabbed for her touch again.

She hesitated

    then,

    took my hands again.

The surge of energy ripped

through us and

I felt myself bubble up

With laughter, the girl joined me

And we spun each other around

        And around.

In the fallen leaves

The ones that our power knocked off their trees.

    This energy was beautiful.

It allowed me to smile

wider than I ever have.

I was happy, actually

                         Happy

Dancing with the core of

                              our beings

                                             I thought

I would never be this happy,

but I was mistaken.

     We fall to the ground and

both of us giggle. I

To the girl, smile.

     "Thank you."

She smiled and then

laughed a puzzled chuckle.

"Why thank me?

We don't know each other."

But I felt like I did.

I sat up and shot my hand

out for her to take.

She sat up

took my hand

gingerly,

"My name is Wanda. Wanda Cannon.

What's yours?"

Her pause was minimal

A light growing warmth between us.

"Gemma. My friends call me Gem for
short."

We let loose our hands.

"Well, it's nice to meet you, Gemma."

"Likewise." she laughed.

"I must say it's intriguing to see you

in this part of the jungle.

Where'd you come from?"

I thought I was the only one.

I looked at her, my face

contorted; I wasn't sure.

"I don't really know. I just

kinda showed up."

I'm the next one to question her.

"Where'd you come from?

Are you alone?"

Like me?

My head starts to dim

Can't focus on the things

around me. I barely catch

my new friend, Gemma,

> *walking away*

and back the way she went.

I call to her,

My nerves tearing through me

> *once again.*

> *"Wait! Gemma, where—*

> *where are you going?!"*

She pops her head back,

> *Shushing me.*

> *"Stay there. I'm gonna be right back. I'm going to return*

with my friends.

They'll want to see you."

I nodded my head

sitting quietly.

Gemma wasn't alone

and I

was about to meet her friends.

The wind was rushing

whistling past me.

It shrouded me in a cloud of dust

I have to close my eyes

refrain from any of it getting in them.

My breathing becomes deep

slow.

I could faintly hear the leaves

blowing through the constant,

                            Power

A tornado is around me. It's

                 peaceful.

I felt at ease

in the chaos I laid

On the ground pushing,

My hands and feet in the raw soil.

It was cool and made my body

                               frail

I felt the goosebumps pop,

                    up on my arms, my legs.

                  "Wanda!"

I turned sharp to my name

The chaos died in a moment

I stood frazzled

wiped the dust off my uniform

stared at the area Gemma had disappeared in,

Hoping to see her reappear.

    "Gemma?"

The silence became unnerving.

    "Gemma, where are you!?"

                    I yelled.

A moment passed

Gemma strode out of the bushes,

              three girls—who seemed

all around the same age as Gemma and I—followed behind.

"Wanda?"

I looked to Gemma,

questioning. She looked confused

pale in the face.

"Gemma, what's wrong?"

I went and

touching her shoulder,

She flinched away. She

looking everywhere except

in my eyes.

I was

right in front of her

It looked like I was completely invisible.

Like she was seeing right

through me.

"Gemma?   Can you hear me?"

She touched her hand to

        The place my hand still rests.

                I see her shiver.

                        "I can still feel her."

"Who?"

Both of us turned

one of her friends,

        The one in the middle,

                She seemed like the leader

the group

                she held them tall.

                "Who are you talking about,

because no one is

here

except us.

Are you just doing this to get back at me?"

"What? No!

I'm not that sort, and deep down

you know that,

Alice!"

"Okay then, Gem."

The one on the right of Alice.

She was short

terrifying all the same.

"Say you're speaking the truth. What, or

. . . who are

you talking about?"

I felt my chest tighten,

my legs began to give.

I didn't know what was

happening but I was calm,

if I knew deep,

        deep down

                I was safe.

My breath became hard

My lungs not taking in

air as it was before, I collapsed

to my back, the ground warm

I tried to grab at the soil

                Below me,

nothing came up.

It felt like someone

holding me down;

a hefty force.

My eyes were straining

on everything around

As if I was being physically pulled

My sweet dream!

I turned my head

Gemma!

focusing all my energy

on her, She gasped.

saying my name,

quick and sharp. She spoke:

"Wanda."

011

INDISPOSED

[WANDA]

"Wanda! Wake up!"

My eyes shot open and I was looking into the face of someone familiar.

Eric. He was on top of me, his arms tightly wound around my back, on the ground. I looked around in a daze, frazzled by the harsh thoughts of flying, then being slammed to the ground by an unknown force.

Did Eric pull me out of my dream?

Could I even really call that a dream?

"What's going on?" I heave. He eases himself off of me and we stand. I swayed to the side and he grabbed my arm to steady me. Grabbing my head in pain I groaned, "everything hurts."

"You mind telling me what *that* was?"

I couldn't remember what exactly happened. My head was spinning too fast. "What, *what* was?"

"You seriously don't know?"

I shook my head. Bad idea. I crouched down, clasping my head in both hands. I squeezed my eyes shut and counted the seconds to when I couldn't feel the pulse in my head pounding in my hands. He reached down and cupped my shoulders.

"Can you remember anything?" He questions.

I whispered, "No, I just remember a sharp pain."

"Well, I guess that's kinda my fault."

"What do you mean?"

"Seeing that you don't remember, I'll just tell you what I saw." I looked up at him. He seemed as if the words he was about to speak were crazy talk. "I came in when you didn't answer. Thinking nothing of the sort, I'm stunned to see the sight before me. I thought I'd find you asleep in here, but rather found a wondrous sight. You! You were . . . Flying! Hovering in the air as if stranded inside of a tornado."

"A tornado?" I shook my head, "That's impossible. Magic hasn't been used for hundreds of years. And even I know that."

"Yeah, I know! I called your name, but you didn't answer. You were asleep! I said to myself she couldn't possibly be doing this, right? So, I decided to try and get you down."

I felt my chest tighten, and my legs began to give. I didn't know what was happening . . .

"So . . . you jumped on me?"

He nodded his head. Astonishment boiling over his green pools. "I pulled you to the ground and in an instant, the wind stopped. The chaos—stopped."

. . . but I was calm, as if I knew deep, deep down I was safe.

"I must have been dreaming."

"Is that what happens when you dream? You—float in a chaotic tornado?" His eyes, his beautiful eyes that make me warm and fuzzy inside, carry the weight of fear in them. *Will he tell Valmore about this?*

I give a weak smile to reassure him. "No. This is the first time. The only time." I pushed his arms gently away and stand. He still looks concerned, but I wave it off. "Why don't we go? I'm sure I'm already late on my first day."

"What about your head? You should give it a rest."

I shook my head, ignoring the piercing thread of pain in my mind. "I'm fine." I smile. Show little teeth as I add, "Really. It was brief and it's already gone."

He opened the door for me and asked again. "Are you sure you're okay?"

"One-hundred percent sure. If I don't feel well, I'll tell you." I lied.

If he thought I wasn't okay, he'd tell Valmore. He'd rush in here to see what all the commotion is all about. General Underwood as well. I'd be put on more medication. Meds would take hundreds upon thousands of examinations and tests to see why I did what I did. See what makes me tick. I wouldn't be able to handle it anymore.

I need to figure this out on my own. See why I have powers; an energy that flows in every molecule of air. And why I can talk to people through my dreams--if they're even real.

I need to train. Build my body to not only strengthen my limbs but my powers. *I won't be able to fight my own battles if I'm strapped to my bed and left to rot for another seven years.*

I'd be useless.

Eric gave a hesitant nod and closed the door behind us. I didn't bother to turn and lock the door. I didn't want to look into those eyes again. Not when I might give up and tell the real truth--that I was absolutely terrified of what happened and absolutely exhilarated at the same time.

012

PRACTICAL

[ERIC]

I had left her room, telling her I'd be back in the morning. She'd waved me off with sleepy eyes--so soft in the fits of exhaustion--and drifted off to sleep faster than I could tell her "Good night."

I pushed her really hard in training today. Not because she was behind Valmore's schedule, but because I wanted to see her crack. It had been clear this morning she wasn't fully ready. Especially after I'd pulled her to the ground in a bear grip because somehow she had powers that made her fly.

I was used to seeing individuals with magic after all--my neighborhood back home was littered with them, even though it was against the law. They would get exhausted--the kids especially--when they used them excessively. I knew this was the case for Wanda when she said she was fine.

She clearly wasn't. I could read it all over her--the way her form would relax and tense after every step. The way her smile tightened more than normal.

She had started to get more comfortable the more I stuck around, but to see her exact emotions without much effort anymore, nagged at me. She concentrated in training, yes, but still . . . I couldn't help but wonder, *What was she hiding?* When Valmore came in after dinner, she tensed up like she normally would when he came. More tense this time, possibly thinking I had told him what happened.

But when he didn't ask anything other than the usual line: "How has she performed today?" I looked at her with a tilt of my head.

I had said my normal line, "She's excelling on schedule, sir."

And then he said: "Perfect!" and he'd be out of the door faster than I could nod my head.

Everytime, Wanda would be standing with her bed between us, her hands fisting her sweats as if to keep herself from launching into action. Again.

That was my que it seemed--my only mission now, to bring her food from the cafeteria. I'd check her room first before moving onto where I knew she'd be.

Her hiddy-hole.

She'd go there before anything else.

"Why haven't you told Valmore about this place yet?" she had moved her legs up to hug them to herself. "Is this your sick and twisted way of blackmailing me if I do something wrong?"

I avoided her gaze as I pushed my tray to the side. "How do you know I haven't already told him?"

The space around us was quiet. We were the only ones who could listen to each other's slow breathing. "You're different," she had said.

Different how? I didn't know how to respond. It could have meant anything. I was different because of the way I treated her compared to Valmore. I was different by the way she could never truly trust me because she could be planning to trick me to get out, or that I might throw her under the bus for my own personal gain.

My personal hope: I was different because both of us trusted each other more than we could admit to the other. She's trusting me more than she wants to, and I'm trusting her because everytime I ask why I'm doing this, I think back to my sister. They're so much alike, and yet not. So when I think I know Wanda, I'm thrown down a totally different path to adventure.

Ever since I told her my name, she's been calmer. Less unnerved by my presence. Enough to not send her immediately running for her hiddy-hole. And before today, I thought she'd been lying about it being a courtyard to hide something more daring. But she wasn't. *She wasn't lying at all.*

Why is she lying about not feeling okay, then?

"Well, well, well. Look who's finally showing his face. It's Eric Florbal, everybody!"

I'd finally walked all the way back to the barracks. This made it my second night coming back later than normal. The first being the night of the stupid Meilo Party.

"Whatta you want, Kane?" I groaned. The bags under my eyes were growing heavier, I could feel.

"Oh nothing!" he chuckled. "I'm just thinking about all the extra time you've been spending with Cannon has already started to pay off. Seeing how she obeys your every order and all, today. She must've given herself to you several times by now. Quick lad."

I roll my eyes and push past him. He grabs my shoulder.

"You've gotta tell me. Is she just as hot without her clothes as she is with only a sheet covering her?" He's thinking about Petition day. She'd only had a thin gown under the surgical towels.

The thought of her needing a blanket to keep her warm, came flooding back. Now, she sleeps with all her sweats on. Including her socks. *Could this be the reason?*

I shake my head, pity flooding me. "I'm too tired for this conversation right now, Kane."

"I bet you're tired. Tired from all those hot moves today on the matts--"

"Kane!"

Both our heads turned to the voice. Brooks--our senior officer--was at the front of the hall, both his hands mounted on his hips.

He looked between us before settling back on Kane. "My office. Now."

He cursed under his breath, adding, "See you later, Florbal."

I tilted my head in a silent thanks to Brooks as I turned back around. "Not likely," I countered under my breath.

013

SHIFTED

[WANDA]

Two weeks passed like a snap of my fingers; it filled with routine and nothing else.

I'd wake up at three o'clock every morning from another lucid dream.

Why I couldn't accept that my dreams were just merely dreams, I don't know? And why it had to be the same scene every time, as if I could get back fully to the place I was before with that Gemma girl and her friends, I really don't know.

Then, I'd shower—put on my training uniform—and wait in the courtyard for Eric to show up. Since that morning, the one where I was supposedly flying, Eric has taken it upon himself to show up early in the morning so I don't have an "accident" again. Though I knew it wasn't just an accident, I didn't bother to tell him that. I didn't want to give him any reason to worry more than he already had to.

I can see it in his eyes. The way he wants to protect me when I crack under the pressure.

After doing a little hand-to-hand combat together, we'd head off to do some "actual training" as he called it.

That's when I'd see it. The emotions flooding through his glowing green pools. His face doesn't give him away, but if someone were to really look deep into his eyes, they'd see. They'd question.

Only a couple of soldiers dare come close when I practice. Most steer clear, giving me a scornful glance as they leave. But I guess I can't complain. It makes more room for the training I do every day. Gives me more time to do hand-to-hand combat as well as offense and defense training.

Two soldiers come more often than not, Sarah and Brooks--based off the names on their tags. I don't know their first names. They're the ones that stay the longest. And I learned why one night when they invited me to join them in the cafeteria for dinner.

Apparently, they don't follow General Underwood's orders like everyone else.

It made sense then, why no one wanted to be in the same room, let alone train with someone like me. The one who single-handedly took down their leader. Their General. Their mighty protector! Or whatever they think he is. I don't care. I know who he really is.

A monster.

After dinner, Eric would walk me back to my room. His warm smile, the only thing able to break down the wall I spent all day building up between us. *I couldn't help but want to trust him. His words, his actions. But he always seemed one step farther away from me the more we spent together.*

What was he holding back?

Finally, I'd change into my sweats and take the cup with my medication inside. I'd dump them into my stash sock. No Meds had come by to check on me in a while. Neither had Valmore. His trust for Eric was enough to keep him away. I hadn't seen him since my first day of training. *Why could that be?* I wasn't complaining, but it itched at the back of my mind every night before I closed my eyes.

I turned out the lights and climbed into bed. I release a sigh and thank the ceiling above me. I didn't fully know if Eric was the one who kept Valmore away for this long, but all the same, I couldn't trust him entirely. For what, I don't know yet.

014

THE DAY AFTER THE MEILO PARTY

[ERIC]

Callie confessed to me one night that there was only one fighter who could beat her time and time again in the ring. I asked for the name, but all I heard from her murmuring lips were Crusher Cain. Could that have been a stage name the fighter used?

From "My Thoughts / Secrets"--
SRP

Two weeks before . . .

I hadn't felt comfortable leaving Cannon--I mean, Wanda--back with Valmore. But he said I had some files waiting for me on his desk that I just had to read. He told me to take my time since he was going to be at the hospital for a while anyway.

So, I decided to make a detour back to the barracks to take a shower. Lord knows I needed one with the night I just had. The sun was setting when I entered the barracks and the night was back when I left.

Kane tried to converse with me, but I told him I was on duty and I couldn't talk. *I'd rather not talk to him for the rest of my life, thank you very much. Including that smug face of his. All high and mighty.*

Valmore's office was the only one left lit up in the main building behind the Grand Hall. Eerie as ever.

Closing the door behind me, I pulled at the files that lay neatly in the middle of his desk. His monitor is off like usual so I flick on the lamp to illuminate the space in front of me.

There's two files: the first reading **UNDERWOOD, CALLIE H..** The second, **HARRINGTON, DEAN J..**

Cannon's friends from the Meilo party. These are their files.

There's a loud ringing that startles me out of my trance.

I must've dozed off. The phone on Valmore's desk was ringing. I looked around thinking there was someone here to get it. I'm the only one.

"Valmore's office, Florbal speaking."

"Where's Nick?"

Straight to the point, aye? "Not here." I yawn.

"Who is this?"

"Florbal, sir. Nic--Valmore has stepped out for the next couple of hours. Can I take a message?"

I rub my eyes. There's little static as I think the line has been cut short. Then,

"Florbal, is it? Get to my office pronto."

"Who is this?" I yawned again.

"Do not play games with me, soldier!"

His voice immediately veered through conscious thought. "Oh my word, sir, please forgive me--I haven't been--,"

"Enough with the excuses. Get to my office."

There was a pause between General Underwood's voice and mine. I didn't know what else to say.

"Now!" he screamed.

"Yes sir!"

"Come in!" General Underwood's voice rang.

I didn't hesitate to open the door. Closing it behind me, he pointed to a chair in front of his desk.

"Sit."

"Can I ask what this is about, sir?"

Footsteps echoed outside his door. It opened a moment later to reveal Wanda's friends, Callie and Dean. Behind them stood Brooks, his face colder than normal.

Had they provoked him in some way?

I stood to make room for both of them to sit.

Callie was the first to speak, her eyes glancing over me. "I see you brought back-up this time."

I tightened my jaw. Looked at General Underwood as he stared at her. Her face was familiar, now that I'd read her file. One of the many fighters from Omega's Bar. All underground fights went through his joint, no name unmarked. She was a frequent client *and* contender.

"He's not back-up. He's here to observe." he pushed back into his chair, relaxed. *Always his sign that he was ready for anything that was about to happen, if anything should.* "It seems today has proven to be a rocky one. Not only have you embarrassed me in front of my men, but the high court as well."

There was no missing the bashed face. Cannon really hit him with everything she had. He had a solid black eye and a broken nose, the wrap around it puffy from all the swelling underneath.

"Like you didn't deserve it, uncle. You treat us like children when clearly we're not."

He gave an eye roll. "You read the papers," he paused.

"Yeah, and I'm still not buying it. What King wants to commend two randos from the streets, and offer them a job as new trainees for his army? That's some messed up bull--,"

"Cal!" Harrington piped at her. "That's enough."

"Even you should--!"

He shook his head. *This guy was commendable. Smart.*

What was he hiding?

Callie ignored the gesture and pushed on. "If we're winners or whatever, why are we here? Why aren't we there?"

In the capital with the King and his army? We had the

same unconscious question. I wondered the same thing. *Why weren't they there instead of here?*

I knew it was something I couldn't question deeper. General Underwood made everyone clear of that.

"He wants you here, that's why. Says I train the best men on the east side. Doesn't want to mess it up. His words, not mine."

There's an eye roll. "What about Wanda then? She can't be here anymore. She needs to go home."

"Home to where? Her parents died years ago. She has nowhere else to be but here."

Callie slumped back in her seat. She looked defeated physically. But her eyes showed a burning determination. "What do you expect us to do then? Obviously we can't interfere with Wanda's work, or whatever that Vik dude told us. You expect us to train with your men or something?"

"Precisely."

"Then why don't we make this quick. If I can take down your most skilled fighter, then we can leave. All three of us. For good."

The file said she had a gambling problem. Yeah, more like

a death wish if you ask me.

"Does that seem like a fair wager? Huh?" Underwood was glancing at both Brooks and I with his one good eye. Brooks laughed, said: "I'd watch that."

I hesitated. "He's not the cleanest player, so I wouldn't call it fair."

She gave me the coldest glare. "Who said a fight had to be fair?"

General Underwood let out his famous bass chuckle. The one that read, "*Oh, you wanna play that game do ya?*" and landed you halfway in your own grave. "Let's make it a challenge then. If you win, I'll let all three of you leave." he leaned up and onto his desk with clear excitement. "But if my soldier wins, not only do all three of you stay here, but that soldier will be your official guide."

"Guide to what?" Harrington questioned.

"Guide to--he'll be your personal babysitter for me."

Babysitter, Valmore. I told you!

Callie's face lit up like a festive tree. Stuck out her hand for Underwood to take swiftly in his. "You've got yourself a deal."

Three weeks later...

Of course, I was the one running away again. Running away from my problems.

"Don't stop until you get her somewhere safe. Promise me. She has to be safe."

Why was I always so scared? The only people I cared about in this world were in trouble.

Why am I so scared?

"I won't do this without you. She needs you. I need you."

I thought I was strong enough to stand up to my bullies at the Meilo party. I thought I could fight for Callie, Wanda, *and* myself. But then Wanda stepped up to the plate before me. Took the bullet for me (figuratively of course).

Now we're all separated again. Because of *me*.

I never should have taken those files without some security in mind. How stupid.

Not this time.

"It has to be you, Dean. Save me later."

This wasn't the end. All of us could get out. Together.

I let loose a weak smile. "Don't give them a chance. Not a single one. Got that?"

"Loud and clear." she grinned, "Now, take these," pushed files into my chest, then kissed my cheek, "and run."

This was my only mission. I couldn't mess it up this time.

Not this time.

I didn't look back. Even when her screams erupted.

Not this time. Not again.

The hospital was dark. No abundance of people in sight.

"It *has* to be you, Dean."

A radio came to life a hall away. I dipped into the shadows until the soldier passed. There were no doubt a couple more patrolling around the building. Wanda was here, somewhere. But where?

"She's in room 1270B." Callie had said.

How am I supposed to know where that is?

Over here, Dean.

I looked around. No one but me.

I'm over here!

Wanda. It's her voice.

How's that her voice? I know it's her. She's pointing me in the right direction.

"Okay, Wanda, show me the way." I whispered. Her voice echoed through my head. Pulled my body forward faster than I could run toward her.

Almost there . . .

There it is! Room 1270B, just like Callie said.

My eyes spotted the new patrol coming this way, a flashlight in hand. His radio was sticking close to his ear as I dipped around a pillar. It's now or never. More static sounded and I slipped quietly behind him. As he rounded the end of the hall, I was already closing Wanda's door behind me.

THIN WHITE LIE

[DEAN]

I nudged her arms. "Wanda. Wanda, wake up."

"Eric?"

I shook her shoulders with more urgency. "Wanda, you gotta get up for me."

"Five more minutes. I'm trying to get back to my friends."

Did they drug her with something? "Wanda! Get up."

Nothing.

I pulled her arms around my shoulders. "Hold on tight, alright?" she nodded, dipping her head into my shoulder. I pulled her legs around my waist, shifted the new weight on my back.

Time to go.

I checked the blinds. All clear.

"Where are we going?"

I knew she was still asleep. "Just hold on tight--we're almost there."

"Okay," she murmured.

"TSK! Make sure he hasn't reached her yet. That's the first place he'll go."

"Understood. Checking--," the soldier spotted me before I could turn around the entrance desk. *Shit.* "Don't move!" he shouted.

I froze.

"Turn around slowly." he spoke something into his radio as I turned to face him. "Now put the girl down, and walk forward."

I shook my head. "I can't do that."

"You think you've grown a pair since the last time you were here, Harrington?"

I didn't move.

"Hand over the girl."

I looked at his belt. No pistol. No stunner. I was in the clear. "If you want her, you'll have to catch me first."

017

BETRAYER

[ERIC]

The objective was clear: Get to Wanda before Harrington, and make sure he doesn't get away. Plain and simple.

That was five minutes ago.

Now I was running to the front of the building, trying to catch up to them. Harrington had nabbed Wanda a few minutes before I got to her room. Now he was about to get away with her.

I fisted my radio. "Shut the building down. Now!"

I gotta get to her. I gotta get to her!

"There he goes!" a soldier howlered.

"Where?!"

He pointed to his right. "He's heading for the back wing."

I didn't want to believe his words. "Where?"

"He's taking her into the back wing. Into the unfinished--,"

"I got that!"

Both of us were running in pace with each other. "Then why'd you ask?!"

Because that's where Wanda's hide-away is. She's taking him to the one place I can't stop soldiers from venturing. *Damn it, Wanda.* "Run and get Valmore."

"I can't just leave--,"

"That's an order! I can handle it from here." He wasn't stopping. I looked at him. "Now!"

I was running to the only place I could think of. The only place that was safe. Dean made it clear that we needed to get out of here. He had a plan.

That's what he said when I finally woke up from my daze. How I slept through him stealing me away and him being chased with me on his back, I wouldn't know. All I knew was I was awake now. Ready for a real fight.

Is Eric trying to find me?

There was no time to think.

I pushed the door open. "Get in."

Dean slipped inside. I was right behind him. Closing the door, I leaned against it.

"Talk. Now."

Dean was heaving deep breaths. "You're not as light as you used to be. You know that?"

"Dean." I snapped. He looked at me. "What the hell is happening? Where's Callie?"

He shook his head.

"Dean, there's no time to think things through. Tell me what's happening or I'll let the soldiers in."

"Don't!"

"And why not?"

"You can't trust them. None of them."

Eric?

Dean was pulling vanilla folders from under his shirt.

"What are those?"

"Files about us."

About us? "Why do you have them?"

"We found out the truth, Cal and I. Took our chances."

"Chances with what? Getting me out of here? Did you not see how many soldiers were chasing us?"

"Yes, I saw. That's why we need to get you out. Before--"

"WANDA!" Eric's voice. It rang through my skull. He was almost here.

"Dean," I nodded my head to the side. "Help me with the door."

He didn't hesitate. Dug his feet in to prepare for the impending force.

"Where is Callie?"

"Not here."

"Dean, you can't expect me to run along with you without knowing where she is. You know that."

His face contorted as the banging began. Eric's voice was ringing out as were a number of others. "Open the door!"

"Tell me."

He shook his head. "She wanted us to get out before anything was explained. She knew you wouldn't handle it if I told you."

"Clearly she doesn't know me very well."

"We both do. You need to understand."

I shook my head. "Either you tell me, or I step away from the door. It's your choice." I trusted Eric. And I was blocking the door from letting him in! But Dean's my friend too. Why was he so scared? Was he scared of Eric? Why would he be scared of him?

He grudged and slammed his fist into the door. "There's a reason the King chose to come here."

"And why's that?"

"You hadn't seen the posters around town like we did. How can we blame you? You were in a frickin' coma for seven years."

"What posters?"

"The ones about 'Alice and her Renegades'. They're everywhere."

The name--Alice--seemed familiar. *Where had I heard it before?*

The pounding on the door increased. I hissed. "And what does that have to do with anything?"

"What did they tell you you were here for?"

"What?"

"OPEN THE DOOR BEFORE WE BREAK IT DOWN!"

"Answer the question, Wanda."

Valmore told me I was here to finish my trials before I'm cleared to go home. He told me my training was the last step. "He told me I could go home if I passed my last trial. That's it."

He shook his head. "Look."

I grabbed the files out of his hand. Focused on the file with my name on it.

"Page 34. It's on page 34."

I flipped through as fast as I could. Stopped on page 34. I didn't understand any of it. "What is this?"

"It's a transfer form. From base to the capital."

I wasn't understanding. "Okay? But what does this have to do with--?"

"Look at the date. It's the night of the Meilo party that the King was at." He was right. The date was correct. "Check the statement at the bottom of the page."

I, hereby verify all forms concealed and collected under the accords of Country Law, Section 4.1. Transfer is binding and restricted to the new guardian of said person.

"Look at the signatures."

There were four. Three of them I knew. Valmore, General Underwood, and King Peter the Second. The last one was unknown. I didn't know this person--Blake Blackburn.

"This doesn't mean anything. I'm still going home."

His expression was painful. "I want to tell you everything, but we don't have time anymore."

I'm still going home after this. I'm still going to go home and see my parents again. Right?

Right? "What does it mean?" I urged. Dean looked at me. "What does it mean, Dean! Tell me!"

"It means that you don't have a choice in this anymore. They're sending you to the capital."

"For what?"

"Alice and her Renegades aren't just random people.

They're like you and me."

"I don't understand."

"Alice Walker, Leah Barnes, Misty Jones, Gemma Sanders. All of them have powers or special abilities. It goes against the law. They ran from the King. Don't you get that? You're next. The King has been circling up those with powers. Probably to rally up a new army or something."

How'd he know I had powers?

It could have been for the best. I'd be able to date Eric without hiding it. "And how is that a bad thing? I could be a part of something big!"

"You don't get it. You haven't seen what I've seen! You can't be here when he comes back. I . . . ! I can't let him take you!"

His eyes were pleading. I knew that expression. It was the face of knowing. He knew more than he was letting on. How could I trust him? He wasn't telling me all of the truth.

Did Eric know about all this? Surely not. He wouldn't let it happen to me. I trusted him. He wouldn't let anything bad happen to me.

What about the dreams I've been having lately? I could

fly and talk to people in my dreams. That could have meant anything, right?

I had to choose between my friend and the guy I was finally starting to trust.

Silence seeped through my bones. The door had ceased motion.

I turned to Dean with confusion. His eyes were wide.

"GET DOWN!"

There was a constant ringing in my ears as the smoke cleared around me. I could see Dean across from me, his head turned away. I squinted my eyes to look at him closer.

There was a piece of the door lodged into his torso. It was as big as my hand.

I coughed out his name. I couldn't hear myself. Only the ringing.

"Wanda," someone's voice was close. It was muffled, soft. *Was it Eric?*

I couldn't move to see. Everything was stiff. Everything was frozen.

Why can't I move?

"Wanda, can you hear me?"

It was Eric's voice for sure. He kept calling my name. I couldn't answer. Dean's body was stabbed by something sharp. I needed to help him.

Dean. Tears were cooling my cheeks. Dean. Dean! He needs help.

I need to move!

Men were flooding the room. Some had pistols aimed at Dean. Others were watching the figure behind me. I could only see moving lips as my head started to pound. Someone lifted me off the ground.

My head lulled back, my eyes looking up at Eric's. His face was stone cold, but his eyes were raging. Sadness, hurt, frustration, worry.

Was it all for me?

His lips moved. Something, something, clean up. Something something, dismissed.

I wasn't understanding. Nothing was clicking.

What was happening? Where was Dean? Where was Callie? Why was there a ringing in my ears?

Make it stop.

Eric looked down on me, furrowing his brows as he said something quiet.

I asked him to speak up and he didn't respond. He didn't even acknowledge that I ever spoke. I was . . . . . drifting . . .

I felt a shadow cast over me. Cold and warm all at once. Then nothing followed after.

020

NEW COMMANDS

[ERIC]

When I got Wanda back to her room, three nurses were at the ready. All of them were checking for injury. I said, "She's not hurt." and one of them still pushed me aside as Brooks came bounding down the hall.

"Where the hell is Valmore?" I snapped.

"Gone. General Underwood wants to see you."

"I can't leave now."

"That's why I came. I'll watch over her while you're gone."

"You don't understand, she--,"

"It's not a request, Eric."

I huffed. *Damn!* "Then do me a favor. If anything--and I mean *anything* happens--you call me. Got it?"

He let out a smile. "What's the big deal anyway? You got feelings for her?"

"I'm serious."

"And you need to answer my question."

I held back, afraid to admit it. "You can't tell anyone."

"I'm not the person you should be worried about." He pleaded, "Eric, you can't do anything. I won't say anything, but you need to be careful."

"I can handle it."

He shook his head. "I'm serious. Reports are coming in that Blackburn is coming. And when he does, do you really think he'll be happy to see a soldier messing around with one of his test subjects?"

Test subjects? I'd heard that Blackburn was a ranking official to the King. I knew 'Alice and her Renegades' used to be under his command. Reports spoke of an ambush and a wounded official. *Blackburn.*

The stories about him were menacing, but my idea of him was childish at most. He didn't scare me.

"I'll take my chances. Now can you please make sure

nothing happens?"

"I'm serious, Eric. You need to think this through."

I locked my jaw. I knew what he was trying to say. *I need to think about Sonia.*

I never should have told him about her. Even if he was the only one who knew, besides Valmore, he was trying to convince me that what I was doing was wrong. But if I can help Wanda. Save her . . . I could save my own sister. There was nothing wrong with falling in love with her.

Brooks was searching my eyes, then backing away. "I'll make sure you're the first to know."

I released some tension in my shoulders. "Thank you."

He stopped me. "Promise me you'll stop falling for her. It'll end up getting you hurt if you don't."

I shook my head. Funny thing about falling in love with someone; that was the risk I was willing to take. "Then I'll just watch my step."

I passed Kane on my way to Underwood's office. General Underwood's niece--Callie, Wanda's friend--was being hauled away in Kane's arms, kicking and screaming like a toddler. Except, this toddler knew words unpleasant to the ear.

"Close my door." Underwood sighed. As I did, he pulled out a bottle of whiskey from his shelf. "Want one?"

I shook my head, "I'm good thanks."

"Suit yourself." He downed the first shot and poured himself two more before adding, "please, sit."

"What is this about?"

"You asking me that makes me wonder if you've even heard yet."

"I've been busy."

"And might I say your work is bringing Cannon ahead of schedule."

I bit the inside of my cheek. "Is this about what happened today?"

He circled his drink in hand. "Yes . . . and no."

I wasn't caring for the prolonging of this conversation. He was hesitating over something, but I couldn't tell what. He also seemed agitated about something. Or maybe someone. Possibly his niece?

"Where's Valmore?"

"That's what *you're* here for."

I tilted my head. Questioning.

He continued. "Valmore has been given a promotion. Packed up his office and left this afternoon."

The amount of disdain was enough to read that that's what he was more concerned with. "And what does this have to do with me, sir?"

"You weren't my first option. For the "Guide" job, I mean." He used finger quotes. Then, "Valmore was the one who introduced me to your . . . situation."

He said it as if he had re-evaluated my position here when he'd heard of it. As if it was a reputation-damaging thing to be held accountable.

"Though I didn't make the call myself, and it's good that I didn't. You've proven yourself to be quite valuable."

Thank you? "I'm still unsure as to why you called me away from my duties, sir?"

He leaned over the front of his desk, his drink set aside. Forgotten. "I called you in here to notify you of your new position. With Valmore gone, a replacement is needed to look over both a patrol for the girl, and yourself." I opened my mouth to counter and he held his hand up to stop me. "Now, Valmore has given a good word for you and I've read all his reports. You're short and quick with reports, no detail left out.

"That is why I'm letting you take Valmore's place. You'll still go through your day-to-day routines while training with Cannon. Your pay will be upped three times what you've been promised. Not to mention the request you put in some months ago."

I'd put in the request after Petition day. Not even hours after I watched Wanda get poked and prodded did I sit down and write in a week's request of PTO time.

Then it was denied two days later.

"Now, the catch is that I cannot let you use your PTO time until our superior officer comes in. He's been planning to come here for weeks but has been held up with work in the capital. Something about runaways."

Blackburn.

He's the superior official to every base in this sector. Everything that went through this place, went through him first. Every request. Every enrollment.

Every incident.

"When is he expected?"

Underwood shrugged. "I give it a week at the most."

The only thing on my mind was Wanda. "What does this mean for Cannon? If Harrington hadn't provoked her then--,"

He shook his head. "It's none of your concern. Kane has it under control for the time being until Blake gets here."

"But what about after he gets here?"

"Blake's made it clear that no one is to know of his plan until he's here himself. And by that time, you'll be home with your sister."

"But--,"

"It's enough said. That's all I can say until he gets here."

I tightened my jaw. Things didn't seem the way they were said. Underwood was holding something back, and I wasn't sure as to what. "Understood, sir."

He nodded his head. Turned his back toward me to look out his window. The sky was beginning to lighten the next day. "You're dismissed. Get some shut-eye before finishing those reports. They all come to me as of today."

I stood and looked out the window a second longer. Then, I opened his door and closed it behind me, my thoughts too numb to my exhaustion. Sleep was the only thing juggling through my brain as I walked back to the barracks. As I kicked my boots to the ground.

Not a moment too soon did I collide with the soft cloud of heaven that I called my bed, sleep immersing me in a blanket of endless warmth.

021

LASHING OUT

[WANDA]

"You need to calm down." The nurse said. "Your body has gone through a traumatic break--,"

This was the fourth time today I'd started this argument with her. She was getting irritated by it. So was I. "You don't think my friend hasn't either? I need to make sure he's okay."

"And I've told you. For the last time, he's perfectly fine."

I rolled my eyes. The last remembrance of Dean last night was looking at a large chunk of metal lodged into his abdomen. Blood had been pooling under him faster than I could focus on it. Then Eric was taking me away.

I hadn't seen him since last night either. All that I knew was that Brooks was taking his place for the time being. How long that would be, I wasn't for sure.

I looked between him and the nurse. Brooks wasn't gonna

budge anytime soon. "Official orders. Nothing I can do," was his words.

Standing from my bed I tightened my jaw. The nurse was cautious with how close she was to me. "You said that an hour ago. A lot can happen within a span of an hour."

"And nothing has changed. He's resting. End of discussion."

I fisted her wrist. Brooks took a quick step forward. "Either you tell me the truth," I growl, "Or you let me see him."

She looked between my hand and my gaze, shaking her head slowly. Caution was seeping from every pore of her. "Let me go."

"Cannon--,"

"Not until you meet my request!"

She was barely moving. Her response was unmoving. "Wanda, you need to calm down."

She was pulling something out of her pocket. I grabbed her arm. She dropped it. The syringe shattered on the floor. Brooks took me around the middle. My hands were still out-- reaching for her. Any of her.

Her body froze, her throat restricting with an invisible force. "Please," she croaked, "Please, let me go."

I shake my head. Brooks called for help.

"Cann--Wanda, Wanda! Let her go! *Let her go!*" Brooks heaved.

Was I really going to do this? Did I really need to hurt her to get what I want? I shook my head. "I need to know he's really okay."

"He is!" she choked.

My nose burned while my eyes pooled with tears. "You're lying. You're always lying! I saw the blood. I saw the amount."

She shook her head under the restraint and coughed. "Please--!" her eyes were turning red. Her face was turning a vibrant shade of purple and blue.

Then she was falling back. My arms were becoming numb. Something pricked at the back of my neck. I hadn't seen the other nurse come in.

Words became distant. My eyes slumped down.

"--what happened? Why didn't you call me?"

The new voice was too far for me to catch. But Brooks was so close. It was as if he was whispering into my ear. "I was handling it," he said.

"This--you call this handling it--? . . .had the nurse . . !"

"It was the only thing stopping her from killing her. She would've killed her."

"No . . .can't be."

"What would you expect me to do?"

"Anything but that!"

Was that Eric's voice? His voice was still too far to tell for sure.

He seemed so distressed. Was he mad at me?

Eric?

My eyes felt glued shut now. My mind was slowly disappearing.

disappearing.

022

MISDIRECTION

[MISTY]

[She] spoke of individuals in the dreamscape as one of two things:

<u>Lights:</u>
Those who have powers, magic, or supernatural abilities.

<u>Darks:</u>
Those who do not have any powers or special abilities.

In other words, people who are Human. Through and through

The others spoke of it vaguely, but [She] was the only one who really spoke of it in immense detail. She even went on to talk about her first encounter with what she called a "Transparent".

From "My Thoughts / Studies"--SRP

There's one thing I've caught onto when I'm in the dreamscape; The spirits. No matter who enters the space, everyone comes here at some point throughout their lifetime. Some, more than most.

Here, there are two distinctions that separate individuals.

I call them the Lights and the Darks. There aren't any others. No other differentiations.

Except for this guy.

His apparatus was unstable, expanding three times its distance around himself. As if searching. Always searching.

Least I forget, his body was translucent.

Transparent if you will.

Not only did it glow like other Lights, his form was solid black. He was both a Light and a Dark.

Darks can't be seen through. Neither can Lights. But you could see through this one.

Were there more like him?

I kept my distance as I studied him. Made sure he couldn't see me. Or at least I thought I was doing a good job of it. He kept turning and looking at me. Looking into me. As *if anyone can do that.*

He could.

"Why don't you speak?" he had asked. "Why won't you answer my question?"

He was looking for someone. Constantly mumbling her name under his breath.

He couldn't seem to find her.

"Where's Callie?"

His hand had reached for mine. It went straight through. Cold enough to make me shiver in my real body.

"You feel just like her. Wanda. She feels just like this."

Cold?

"So warm," he continued. "She was just with me a moment ago. Can you help me find her?" He began to search the ground. "Can you help me find Callie?"

It seemed his mind wasn't fully here. Just like all the

Darks. They all disassociate from this place when they enter it. They can interact with other Darks, but once they try talking to a Light, their minds seem to lose their train of thought.

Like water flowing over an overflowing glass of water. I'll note this all for later. Then I'll tell the others about it. Especially Alice.

She'll definitely want to know about this.

END OF ENTRY_18 | DREAMSCAPE STUDYING

023

THE FALL OUT

[ERIC]

"Why are you here?"

I'd finally got everything done. It took a couple of days, but all the paperwork, all the new assignments given to me--all of it was done so that I could come here and relax.

I didn't move from my position in the chair. "You should be asleep, you know."

"And you shouldn't be here."

I sighed. "You're mad."

I could hear Wanda's sarcastic laugh under her blankets.

"Is this because Underwood took you off the training schedule yesterday?"

I watched her sit herself on the side of the bed. She shook

her head. "Clearly, you don't know me very well. If I was mad about the training schedule, I wouldn't be mad at *you*."

Okay? "Why are you mad at me? I haven't been here--,"

"That's exactly why I'm mad at you. Not to mention that I found out about the report you sent out to Brooks."

She knew.

A couple nights ago, after I'd crashed asleep, someone had dropped off the new reports for me to sign for Underwood. I had still been in a daze the next morning when I read them. Even when I signed them and sent them back, I didn't fully get the memo until that afternoon when I went to check up on Wanda. And that's when I knew. One of the reports I had signed off on was for the restriction notice that Wanda was under immediate house arrest. Meaning--

"Dean needs me." She spoke.

"You can't leave. Not until--,"

"It's all my fault. I need to see him. He needs me."

I shook my head.

"I'm being serious here, Eric. He's in trouble," I scoffed with an eye roll. There was no doubt he was in trouble for what he did. He stole classified files from the database room. Only top officials on base have access. Now, I was one of them.

She tightened her jaw. I lifted my hands in surrender, and she continued. "I can feel it. I don't know how, but I feel that something bad is about to happen."

I watched her frame as it tensed. Something wasn't right. "You're lying."

She stood. "When have I ever lied to you? Huh? Tell me."

I sighed. I wasn't ready for this conversation yet. It was too late and I was way too tired. "I didn't mean to say it like that. I'm just exhausted."

"Then why are you still here? If you're tired, you shouldn't be bothering me."

She was right. "You're right," I stood from my chair. "I should just go."

I had come here to make sure she was okay. And she was. *I wanted to see her face.*

"Wait."

I turned at the door.

"Why did you do it?"

I tightened my jaw.

"Why did you sign that report?"

I shook my head. I was half asleep when I signed that report. But it was the only memo that I got back that I didn't actually hate. "You really want to know why?" I asked.

"Yes."

It wasn't uncommon to see individuals gain powers that hadn't in the past before. And it wasn't even uncommon to be born with them and not know they were there until it was too late. But it always ends the same.

"I found out you weren't taking your medication."

She took a step back. I nodded my head. "I found your stash. Right under that planting pot you always sat on."

"What did you--?"

"I didn't do anything with it. I threw them all in the trash," I lied.

She sighed with relief.

My heart tightens at the thought. This is how it starts. She's fine for a little while, then she'll become ill again. Once she starts taking the medicine she'll feel normal and stop taking them. The cycle will never stop. Not until she's . . .

"What's wrong?"

. . . dead. "Hm?"

"You're worried about something. What's wrong?"

I shook my head. "It's nothing, really,"

you'll never guess what I did today, brother! I stopped taking my medicine. Can you believe it? I'm getting better, brother! I'm getting better!

"It's just been a long day. I'm sorry that I woke you. I'll come back in the morning."

"Wait--!"

I even talked to the doctor. He says I'm improving faster than ever before.

"Sleep well."

Just wait! When you come back to visit, I'll be all better. I'll be back to myself!

024

SILENT TREATMENT

[ERIC]

The only place she wanted to go was the library. Then she sat in a chair furthest away from me and stuck her nose in a book. She didn't even get up until we had to go back to her room. And by that time, she closed the door in my face, her point clear.

She didn't want me to be around her.

But it wasn't just me. It was everyone.

When a Med would stop by in the morning to drop off her medicine, she didn't even hide the fact that she wasn't taking it. She just chunked it in the trash.

Then the Med would get mad, and I'd have to block their path so that nothing happened. And they'd storm away, curses fuming under their breath. Later I would have to burn their reports.

"Are you seriously giving me the silent treatment?"

It's been five straight days without her talking. And I'd had enough. Blackburn was almost here--based off reports from Brooks and General Underwood. He could be here any day now, and Wanda was still mad at me. I didn't want to go home knowing she'd still be mad at me. I didn't understand what I did wrong?

"Can't you at least say you hate me to my face?"

She closed the book in her hands and stared straight ahead of her for a moment. Then she turned and faced me.

I didn't realize how much I missed looking into her eyes. They were so beautifully gray.

"You're hiding something from me."

My chest tightened. "No, I'm not."

"Yes you are!" she blew up. "Just admit it. You pity me."

"Woah. What?" she had it all wrong. "That's not true."

"Then what is?" She stood from her chair and threw the book onto a side table. "Because you were holding something back the other night. You're mad because I don't take my medication. So what? You really wanna know why I don't take it?

Because it makes me weak. It makes me nauseous, and sick to my stomach every second of every day."

"I'm not mad at you."

She continued. "But when I don't take it--guess what? I feel like I'm on top of the world. I can breathe better, I can stand straighter knowing I won't have to throw up. I can move!"

I tightened my jaw. Frustration was building. "But that's only the start of it, isn't it?"

"The start of what?"

She needed to understand. Understand that, "If you don't take your medication, how do you know you're getting better? I mean seriously. How do you really know?"

"I just know!" She was searching my face. "Why is it such a big deal to you? Can't you trust that without it I'm *better* than okay?"

"No." I looked to the ground, forcing myself not to look at her. Not to see the faces of my little sister and my mother in her. "No, I can't."

"Why not?"

"Because you're not the only one who's gone through

what you have." I pinched my eyes shut and sighed deeply. "My mother and sister are just like you. They have special abilities--,"

"Powers,"

"Yes. Powers just like you. They weren't clear like yours is, but they aren't as strong as you. They're weaker. More vulnerable to the side effects of having abilities."

"What do you mean?"

I hesitated for a moment. *Could she handle the truth?*

"There are a rare few who can go without taking medication for their powers. They are called Masks. But for those who cannot--like my mother, my little sister, and presumably, you--are called The Marked. My mother, one of the Marked, was on and off her medication until the day she died. And the sole reason for her weakened state was her powers alone."

"That's why she was on that medication." she spoke. I looked up at her. "Because without it, her abilities would take over and kill her."

I nodded.

She crossed her arms. "It makes sense."

She was a lot calmer than I thought.

Her head nodded. "When I first turned nine, things started to go downhill fast. My body was weak. I had to take this medication to help me power through most days. I could barely function without it. But then it stopped working."

That's what led her to being put in a seven year coma. Yeah, I read her file. Not only did she move from the best hospital in Hightown, but she was moved here for surveillance.

She had been getting better. Healthier.

"Are you saying I might relapse?"

She was probably reading my expression. I didn't deny she could relapse. But I also didn't say she wouldn't. "I just need you to be careful. I want you to get through this."

She turned away. Back to the book she'd thrown to the side moments ago. "Is that why I'm really here?"

"What do you mean?"

"I mean with all the training and what not. Valmore taught me all the things I missed in school. You teach me how to defend myself. But what else is there?"

Valmore told her that she wouldn't go home until she

finished all his trials for her. But now that he was gone, all that was left to me. And my job is to watch and protect her.

I shook my head. "I don't make that decision."

She plopped herself back into her chair and sighed. "I know."

"And there's nothing that I can do to change anything."

"I know."

"Then why are you so calm about this?" She was completely throwing me off with how calm she was. "Why aren't you mad about that?"

She huffed, standing back up. Her eyes were trained on the door behind me, and I stepped in her path to stop her.

"What are you doing?"

She looked up at me. "I'm leaving. What does it look like I'm doing?"

"Uh, you look like you're about to get into another fist fight with Underwood for yelling at his niece."

Her nostrils flared. "Well, I'm not."

"You're lying."

"Get out of my way."

"No."

"Get out of my way!"

"No!"

"You either move, or I move you myself."

"Either you calm down here, or you tell me what you're actually gonna do."

"Now you're just copying me."

"Or maybe, I'm trying to be the voice of reason."

She huffed, "Augh! Just get out of my way already!" and then she pushed my chest.

I took a step back to make space between us, and she got closer. Fiercer. I felt a sharp breeze whip around me. I could see her fists clenching.

"Wanda, don't do this. You need to calm down."

She shook her head. "My parents are gone! They're gone and I didn't realize it until now!" She was heaving in a sharp breath before a ragged sob broke to the surface. "How could I have been so stupid!"

I scrunched my brow. This was the way I felt when my mother passed away. I felt so lost.

Alone.

"Don't say that. You couldn't have known. There's nothing that can stop that kind of thing."

"Death? I could have stopped it by being there. I should have been there!" she shoved at my chest again and again. "You need to let me go! I need to go home! They need me home!"

"They're already gone, Wanda. You need to calm down. You need to stop this."

Her sobs were shaking her frame. She seemed to be breaking all the way to her very being. "You knew, didn't you!"

I shook my head.

"And you didn't tell me!" She continued, "How can I trust you!"

"I didn't know! I thought you already knew."

Hiccups were sucking up the hot air around us.

"Please," I pressed on, "You need to calm down. You need to stop this chaos."

She shook her head again. "There's no stopping it when it starts. You need to let me out."

I shook my head. I reached out my hands to grab her. "You just need to calm yourself down."

She pulled away. "No!"

The wind around the room was thrashing books across the room. A lot of them were starting to fly off the shelves. She wasn't calming down.

"Wanda," I grabbed her close. Her arms were pressed into my chest and her head was bowed under my neck. "Focus. You need to focus on your breathing. That's how you'll get through this. Focus on slowing your breathing."

"Let go." she whimpered.

I shook my head, "Not until you focus."

The wind became hot. Then it died down. After everything was calm again, I let her go.

"See. That wasn't too hard, now was it?"

Her eyes were closed. As if in deep thought. Her frame was calm again.

"Wanda? You can open your eyes now. Everything's okay."

Her body swayed side to side for a moment before dipping forward.

"Wanda!"

025

DREAMSCAPE

[WANDA]

The smell of dirt brought

my eyes open. I was back

in the small clearing of trees

The air was stale,

      no breeze.

I sighed and turned in a circle.

This was the same place.

The place with those girls.

      What were their names again?

Gemma, Alice and

                    And

            And

Nothing.

                          Alice and her renegades!

I found the familiar area

where I'd first popped through.

The green sea was overwhelming

                    Overgrowing

all over and barely the room to walk through.

I walked straight and hit another clearing.

Same size as the first.

My mind was pooling in disbelief.

        Now--

This had to be true.

I looked around the large clearing

marveling at the thick trees around me.

It was impossible to wrap my arms around the trunk of any of them.

They were too massive.

I call out the first, the

One who spotted me

First.

"Gemma! Where are you!"

My powers, a simple,

powerful

breeze swept by me.

It's so easy here.

My powers flow as easy

As water. As,

Air

My hair blew in my face

obscuring my vision. I--

pulling it back only for a moment--

Swept-back again. The wind was picking up.

and so was my impatience

Growing thin.

I yelled Gemma's name louder,

        Hoping

it would carry on the air.

        "GEMMA! GEMMA, GEMMA! WHERE ARE YOU!"

I wanted her to come out.

        "It's me! Wanda! GEMMA, COME ON!"

I felt the wind push me.

      This isn't me.

      This power isn't mine.

I gritted my teeth, thinking the worst.

What if this was a dream

A playful show for my mind to mangle

                                        I'm
just having false hope. I should have never believed this could be real.

                                        But I
want it to be real.

I cried out her name, "Gemma! Please!"

I heard the faint sound of footsteps

I spun around to see

Someone was walking toward me.

They were sneaking before

I turned to find them.

Their voice was quiet. "Who are you?"

Half her face is painted,

      Deep charcoal

Three white lines marked vertically

      Atop her forehead.

   "I could say the same." I gritted.

The wind was faltering,

dying back to a calm breeze.

I looked closer at the girl

She seemed familiar, felt

her presence familiar.

     I knew her, just

    without her face paint.

"Alice. Your Gemma's friend."

Her stance faltered

sprinted toward me with her hands raised.

Swung a fist at my temple.

I ducked to the side

only jolted back, then

Thrusted to the ground.

She pulled my hair.

straddled me,

my arms under her knees.

"Who sent you?"

"No one, I swear. I just--

showed up."

She trapped my neck. "Lies!"

I shook my head,

nerves surging up,

> down my body.

> "NO! I promise. Gemma will know me. I was the one she was trying to show to you, remember?"

> "When?"

> I swallowed as best as I could. My throat hurt. "Two weeks ago. My name is—,"

"Wanda. I heard."

She stood and held her hand to me.

> I took it and she helped me up. "Then you believe me?"

026

THE RIGHTEOUS PATH

[ALICE]

I *could* believe her.

I hadn't seen a Light other than when I'm here with Leah and Misty and Gemma.

Gemma,

She got this girl into this mess.

Another soul whose life has been thrown into the view of a hawk's eyes.

I couldn't get over how bright her Light was burning. It was gonna get me killed in here.

She repeated herself: "You believe me, right? You can help."

"Help with what?" She wasn't any of my concern. I

had more important problems to deal with than her bugging personality. "There's nothing I can help you with."

"Sure you can!" she pleaded. "My friends and I are trapped here."

Where was "here" for her?

"I mean, you are Alice, right? My friend told me about your cause."

What cause? I felt my anger rising like a mountain behind me. I knew my powers were growing unstable. My shadow was morphing into something monstrous.

Her stance faltered. So did her light. I tilted my head at it as she stuttered along with her words. "I . . . I wasn't looking for trouble. I j-just thought Gemma could help me if she was here. But since she's not, maybe you could help."

I didn't have the time for this. I needed to be on the other side of the ridge right about now. Not--

My breath hitched. Wanda screamed.

I looked down and grabbed at the arrow lodged in my left shoulder.

"You're hit!" She gasped.

I snapped it, leaving the head in the embedded muscle. This was gonna hurt later.

"You're bleeding!"

I pulled her down as another flew past us. "You need to go."

She shook her head. "Not until I get some answers."

I tightened my jaw. Weighing my options was growing harder these days.

"You have strong abilities. Why can't you fight your own battles?"

"I can't control them, my powers. I mean, I almost killed a nurse the other day for just standing there!"

"A nurse?" There were few individuals that I met that were in hospitals. But all of them were severely weak and were unable to cut the connection they had with their Anchor. Where was hers? "Where exactly are you?"

Was she in Hightown like the others?

"I--I can't remember."

"Yes you can," I whispered. I knew both of us could hear

the incoming footsteps. I forced myself to concentrate on only us.

She was flickering in and out of Light and Dark.

I knew what was happening. "You need to listen to me," She was starting to wake herself up. "You need to focus on your powers."

"I can't."

"Yes, you can. You just need to focus on one thing."

"I don't know how--?"

"Focus on me." I gripped her shoulders. "Focus only on me and tell me. Where are you?"

She closed her eyes. Her face was contorted into focus. Her frame became ten times heavier to grasp.

Where are you? I asked in my head.

Silence pulsed between us for several moments. Then,

Here.

The word echoed all around us. Some places it was quiet, others unbelievably ear piercing.

Then it all stopped. A single image entered my mind. One image that formed a memory from a time of my own. Something I wished I would forget.

Only one name stabbed through them both.

Blake.

027

MAKING CONNECTIONS

[ALICE]

"They're coming!"

"And you don't think those Natives aren't coming too! We're getting cornered."

Not only were we cornered. We were pinned down by two forces we couldn't escape from.

One side was blocked by men and women who were solely tasked with hunting us down and bringing us back to the King. The Jay-Hunters, we've nicknamed them now--since it seems we are the birds for predators apparently.

Then on the other side, Natives, which we've recently learned are the real deal. The history books and legends spoke of them. The Aronzoki people. Derived and lived on this land since the beginning of time. Now, hunting any of those who wish to stand, walk, live, or even breathe on their land makes us their soul targets. Even though we've dealt with some of them before-

-we thought they were a myth at the time--, they still do not wish to help those of their own. Even when we're on their side this time.

A plan was needed. And the only best course of action wasn't gonna be the well loved one.

"What we need to do is split up."

Everyone looked at me. Gemma was the first to speak up. "Split up?! Are you absolutely insane? That's not a plan!"

I rolled my eyes. "Gemma, you need to go and find where Wanda is."

She didn't seem to listen. "We're all gonna get caught this way!"

"Gem!" Misty yelled. "Shut your trap already! Alice is getting somewhere with this. Hear her out for once."

Gemma huffed, crossing her arms.

"As I said," I continued, "Gemma is going to find Wanda. Find anything that can help her. And if anything happens, if anyone comes into the picture--."

"I understand." She snaps. "If he comes into the picture, we need to get her out."

"Yes. And no hesitation either. We need to think fast if it comes to it."

I know what I saw from Wanda's memory. She'd shown me her looking at a form. Several unknown signatures were at the bottom, but one was blowing up more than the rest. Even more than King Peter's.

Blake Blackburn.

My stomach dropped to my feet at the thought.

"Good! I'm glad I was clear on that. Now, Leah will deal with the Aronzoki people for now while we think up a tactic to cut them off from us."

"How are we going to do that?" Misty asked.

"I don't know yet."

"Then what *do* you know?" Gemma snapped.

"Nothing? Something? I don't know! All I know is that we need to do this. And you need to believe in me."

She didn't move.

I added, "And if you don't want to believe in me, believe in Wanda. She needs you. She trusts you. You need to be there for her."

She turned away. Her answer: *you're right.*

"Now," I turned to Misty. "Misty. What did you want to tell us? You said you found something a couple of days ago."

"Yes! I wrote everything down in my log book."

"What did you find?"

"I call it a Transparent."

Leah stood from her seat next to me. I was startled.

"A what?" she questioned.

Misty looked between the two of us. Gemma refused to join the group, her back to all of us.

"A Transparent." she repeated. "He was roaming aimlessly around, looking for someone. Or maybe two someones? I don't know."

"Doesn't that just describe a Dark?" I asked. When we first entered the Dreamscape, all we ever saw were Darks--those who couldn't interact or speak to others. Kinda like mindless zombie ants.

She swayed her hands. "Yes and no."

"What do you mean--?"

"I mean--!" She cut Leah off, "He was both a Dark and a Light. You could see through him."

"Hence the nick-name," I nodded. Makes sense.

"Did you talk to him?" Leah asked.

She shook her head. "No. But he tried to talk to me. He kept saying two names over and over again. He was trying to find them, from what I could understand. They were lost I guess." she shrugged. "Then he disappeared."

"What were the names?"

"Wanda and Callie."

That got Gemma to turn around. And all of us looked at each other in a mutual understanding. If this was the same Wanda we were thinking of, then this mission was more important than we all thought. There was no second guessing this. People could have the same names, sure, but I was confident it wasn't a simple coincidence.

This was all coming together.

"Change of plans," I stood. "We need to find a way to get Wanda and her friends out. Now. They're about to get into some big trouble."

028

THROWING ON THE WEIGHT

[WANDA]

My eyes shot open. I'm back in my hospital room, the lights brighter than normal. I squint and look around the room. I spot Eric outside my door speaking to someone. The small wall between the window and the door frame blocks my view.

"How do you feel?"

I look to my right. Callie sits on the side of my bed, clasping my hand. I squeeze it weakly. "Callie? Is it really you?"

Her face cracks open a big smile, her eyes filling with tears. She nods, "Yeah! It's me. I'm so happy you're awake. I didn't think—,"

"Wanda?"

Eric is reaching for my hand. Thinks better when he notices Callie. Holds back. I can see he's full of relief as well.

"How do you feel?"

I give a weak smile. "Not too bad. Can't exactly remember what happened, but--,"

"You fainted." He cut in. "I carried you back here, and caught the eyes of a few passing individuals." he nodded to Callie. I looked at her again as he continued. "She didn't want to leave after she saw you. So I figured having her here with you might speed up the recovery."

"What about Dean?" He wasn't in sight. "Where's he?"

"Resting." Callie sighed. "He's been on bed rest for the next week or so until his wound heals."

So he is okay.

"Underwood! Let's go!"

All heads turned to the soldier at the door, his spiked blonde hair enough to describe his personality.

Callie stood, tightening her jaw and her stance. "He can wait a couple minutes longer, Kane. Quit being a stick up my ass."

"Enough." Eric ordered. "I'll tell her. Just hurry up and go."

I pleaded with Eric's gaze and he turned away. He continued with, "And don't let me regret letting you stay here as long as you did. General Underwood will already have enough to say to me. Don't let me place it all on you."

Callie huffed, fisting her hands. "Fine. But don't think for a second that I won't kick your ass if I find out about another incident like this, and I wasn't told about it first."

"Fair enough."

She looked down to me another moment longer. "I'll see you soon, okay?"

I nod my head. I couldn't promise anything anytime soon. Then she was off, squeezing past the soldier—Kane as she called him—at the door, both of them disappearing down the hall.

"What was that all about?" I asked after they left.

Eric was already sitting on my bed, his hand wrapped around mine. We were finally alone. "Seriously, Wanda. You scared me back there. What happened?"

I furrowed my brow. I really couldn't remember. The only thing that was coming up was—

"Our conversation. You were talking about your mom and your sister."

He avoided my eyes for a moment. When they were back, they were filled with grief.

"You said your mother passed. What about your sister? Is she—?"

"No. She's still at home resting."

"Why aren't you with her? She needs you more than me."

He shook his head. "I can't." He sighed. "That's what your friend was gonna tell you. A superior official is coming onto base tomorrow. You've been invited to join General Underwood and your friends for a private dinner party at General Underwood's house tomorrow evening."

I was confused. "What does this have to do with you?"

"After he arrives, I'll be going home for a week to see my little sister. " he squeezed my hand. "And he'll be taking my place while I'm gone."

My eyes widened. Oh.

"I can't leave until he gets here. That's the only way I can handle work here, and pay to get my little sister the right treatments she needs."

That's why he's not with her. He needs the money. "I

guess the treatments are expensive, huh?"

He nodded. "Yeah." he rubbed the back of his neck. "And to be completely honest with you, you might be the key to her recovery."

"Why do you say that?"

"Because the treatments and training have been the key to your strength. You've improved more than anyone could have thought."

"So, where are you going to take her? You're not gonna be bringing her here are you?"

He shook his head with a laugh. "Not in a million years." he looked at me for a long moment and cleared his throat. "No, I, um--I've been saving up for the last year so that I can take her to the best place in all of Sinitallious."

I tilted my head. "Where's that?"

"Hightown. It's in between Grova and the capital, Herivera."

I heard of them in my studies with Valmore once before. He told me I was transferred halfway through my coma from Hightown to here. I must've driven through the capital to get here.

"I bet it's beautiful down there in the winter time."

When our training began, it was late summer time. Now the fall air was turning bitter. Winter was getting closer and closer by the day.

"I bet it is too. Some of the winter flowers are starting to come out and bloom apparently. At least, that's what my little sister told me in her last letter."

My heart sank at the thought of their distance apart. "Will you give her my well wishes when you see her?"

His face lifted into a warm smile. "Of course. She'll be excited to hear that."

I smiled. "Good."

Eric patted my hand before standing. His hand left mine and shoved them in his pockets. "Now, I'll let you get some rest. I'm sure you need some more before tomorrow."

I nod my head, sinking back down into my pillows.

He turned for the door after a moment longer and I reached out my hand saying, "Wait! I want . . . I want to apologize for what happened a couple days ago."

He turned back, eyes locked in on mine.

"I should have respected your reasons for being frustrated with me. I know you just want the best for me. I understand that now, and I'm sorry. I want you to know I'll always be here. Nothing bad will happen to me. Not anymore."

He grinned ear to ear. "Apology accepted."

"And I also want to add that if I *do* feel as if something isn't right, you'll be the first to know."

He nodded his head, tension releasing all over his frame. "See you tomorrow, Wanda."

"See you tomorrow."

029

TWO STEPS FORWARD

[WANDA]

[They] finally told me the two ways of how others can stun individuals with powers.

1. ONE, Meds (doctors) have ways to push the body into a coma-like state to immobilize the individual into not using their powers.

2. TWO, by medication, simply put. Bonds between "neutral genes" can stabilize the unstable bonds in a charged individual. A compound with chemicals and narcotics mixed within can bring a calm and stable individual. [Their] words. Not mine.

From "Mixed Studies"--SRP

The day seemed to fly faster than the breeze.

Eric had brought over breakfast and lunch for the day,

and we sat in my room for most of the day just talking. He'd occasionally ask if I was feeling any better and I'd give him the same answer; "I'm feeling better now that you're here."

Then he'd smile and go on to talking about how excited he was to see his sister. He told me her name was Sonia. *What a beautiful name*, I thought.

Apparently, in the last letter she'd sent, she had stopped taking her medication. She even went on to say that she was better than ever before and that she couldn't wait to see her big brother again.

I smiled at the thought. I never did have siblings, but I always felt my friends were the closest things to having them. I'd had a crush on Dean when I was little but that was only short lived for the fact that I cared for him more as a friend than someone I'd want to spend the rest of my life with. That includes Callie as well. Now my parents were gone.

For good.

Callie and Dean were all that I had left now.

Could Eric be a part of it too, I had thought? Quite possibly so.

Once all our food was gone, he had to go for one last route check with General Underwood. Then he was back several hours later, picking me up for the dinner party I'd been so graciously invited to.

"Here we are." Eric gestured to the door.

It was the only house on base, sitting on the complete opposite side of where the hospital would be. *It makes sense why I didn't ever see it.*

"Will you say Hi for me when you see her?"

He smiled. "Yes, I'll be sure to tell her." Then he reached across and knocked on the door for me. "Will you promise not to get in another fist fight?" there was a break, "You'll keep your cool?"

I rolled my eyes, hearing footsteps nearing the door. "I promise," I whispered.

"Good," the door opened to a familiar face. "Because I'll be back before you know it."

"Florbal," Kane nodded to him.

"Kane," Eric nodded back. "I'll be sure to mark your reports when I get back."

"Understood, thank you."

Eric and I shared one last glance before he turned away, stepping off the porch and walking away.

I moved past Kane just as Callie did yesterday and nodded my head in respect to his space. "Where's Callie?"

Kane refused to look at me as he spoke. "Up the stairs, down the hall, last door on your left."

I scrunched my brow. "Thanks."

I walked past the loft area around the balcony of the second floor and dipped around the corner of the long narrow hall. "Callie," I whisper-shouted. "Where are you?"

The farthest door came ajar as Callie's head popped through. She smiled, waving me over. "Come on. He's finally waking up."

I rushed forward, pushing to make room for myself. Dean was in bed, his head lulling to the side as his eyes squinted open.

"Dean?" I croaked.

He became conscious the moment he saw me and I

smiled as he said, "Wanda? Is that really you?"

"I'll go get some water."

I turned to see Callie dash off.

"Is it really you?" he repeated.

I nodded, walking over to sit on the edge of the bed. "Yeah, it's me. How are you feeling?"

"I have two bruised ribs at the moment. So, I've been better."

I let out a weak laugh. "How's the wound? Is it all healed up yet?"

He pushed himself to sit up. Then he looked into my eyes. Searching.

"Callie told me."

I was confused. "She told you what?"

"Word went around about you choking a nurse without touching her. Not to mention what happened yesterday in the library."

"You heard about that?"

"How could I have not heard about it?"

I felt I needed to go on the defense. "Well it was *your* fault for all of that happening."

"That's all on you."

"Yeah, because I was worried about you!" I punched his arm. "You left me worried half to death because you just had to tell me something. How stupid can you be? You could've died that night."

It was my turn to search his eyes. And at the point of him breaking down, Callie was walking back into the room.

"There's a reason why we wanted to get you out." Callie countered. "And those files that we had for you were the key to you coming with us."

"I know."

"No, you don't understand. We had to get you out of this place because--,"

"Because you wanted to take me home. I know."

"But--,"

I dipped my head, closing my eyes. "I know my parents

are dead, Callie."

Dean choked on some of his water. "How did you--?"

I shook my head. "Does it really matter anymore? All you guys did was lie to me. You didn't tell me about my parents. You didn't tell me I had powers."

"How were we supposed to know that you had superhuman abilities?" Dean prodded. "You were hauled off when we were ten!"

"We were only trying to protect you," Callie added. "You have to understand that we didn't know what you'd do if we told you about your parents. We don't really understand the whole parent-child-relationship thing."

Because they didn't have them either. And they've been living on their own without them longer than I have.

"None of it matters anymore. I know you guys are my family."

And families stick together, right?

"That's why we want you to leave with us." Callie started.

I looked up at her. Shook my head. "I can't leave Eric here."

She rolled her eyes. "He's just gonna get in the way. He's a threat."

"No, he's not."

"Who's Eric?" Dean prodded.

Callie waved it off. "We can't trust him."

I fisted my hands. "I trust him more than you."

"Yeah," she scoffed, "because he's in love with you maybe."

"He needs my help."

"You can't trust him."

"He's protected me though. Kept secrets from your uncle."

"Woah, woah--wait!" Dean cut in. Both of us looked at him. "Is this the guy that we found in the Database room?"

I gave a confused look. Callie nodded. "He's the one we can't find any information on."

"Wait, what do you mean?" I asked. That didn't seem right.

"He's your guide, right?" Callie questioned. "I could only

assume that with the way he lingers around you constantly. Not to mention the way he looks at you."

I nod.

Dean went wide-eyed. "It all makes sense now."

"What does?"

"That's why we're here." Callie pointed to Dean as she spoke, "That's why you couldn't find anything on him."

"One of you needs to start talking."

"The laws." Dean spoke. "The laws. There had been some put in place a long time ago to restrict magic users. But none of it really affected anything until a year ago."

"So? What does this have to do with Eric?"

"It doesn't just have to deal with him. It has to deal with all of us. When some of the new laws were passed, a lot of people had started to fall off the grid. People were going missing."

"Not a lot of people at first of course," Callie added, "But it grew the more that time went on."

"There had been a rumor spreading about this group of rebels causing disruptions all over the country." Dean hinted.

"And that got me thinking about your case."

I gave him a strange look.

He dismissed it promptly. "On top of all that, another rumor had moved through the crowd. Something about recruiting for special benefits. I hadn't thought of it as anything but a fraud, but then more people were enlisting into the King's army apparently. People who never came home from boot camp after leaving."

"None of this is making sense." I said. "What does this have to do with us?"

"It has to do with everything." Dean shifted straighter in bed. Callie moved to sit next to him, right across from me. We were all so close to each other again. It felt calming.

"Everyone across the country had to follow new testing protocols."

"What kind of testing?"

"The kind that's slowly dividing this country in two."

I looked at Callie. She rolled her eyes. "He's exaggerating. To put it simply; everyone had to be thoroughly tested for any ailments of magic. Depending on the severity, they would be removed and relocated to a different sector."

"But that's a lot of sectors to go through."

She nodded. "Hence why people were going "missing." A lot of people were enlisting into forces trained in treating those with abilities. Meds, nurses, officers, soldiers. You name it."

"Were their records being erased?"

"Some," Dean carried on. "But only those who had something to hide."

"Like what?"

"I did some digging on a lot of individuals. Most of which still reside in the fabled city of Hightown."

Hightown. Eric was going to be taking his little sister there. Was it not safe?

"In my mission to find you, not only did I learn something new, I also found the gruesome truth of the King's true intentions for you and anyone like you." he paused to set his glass onto the side table. "We know the Meds make you take medication to suppress your powers. Do you still take it?"

I shook my head no. Neither does Sonia.

"Good," they both nod. "Not only will that medicine suppress you. It'll also kill you."

"What do you mean?" I shook my head. "Eric said his mother died from having powers. It wasn't the medicine."

"Eric's mother had powers?"

"Yeah," I nod, "So does his sister. But she's better."

"What about him?"

I shook my head. "No. But,--I knew taking my medication was weakening me, but--why does the King have a part in this. He can't be the bad guy here."

They looked at each other.

"Can he?"

"Why do you think 'Alice and her Renegades' are a thing? They ran from his cause. They ran from him."

"Why?"

"You've heard of the Aronzoki people, right?"

"An ancient ruin of the Monster Era." Valmore taught me everything I needed to know. It was only a story, he had said. "How is that important to the King? The history books said it was gone. Only a legend."

He shook his head. "Not quite. The Aronzoki people still thrive there. The Temple still stands as it had a thousand years ago when it was first built. King Peter wants what he can't get. And that's its power. Those who wield it can take over the world if they want."

"And, 'Alice and her Renegades' are the key to that power? We," I pointed between the three of us, "are a part of that?"

"Yeah, and a few hundred others across the country. Those who can--as it was put--travel to the Native Forest without trouble can also connect to the power of the Temple itself. It's where it's been shown to have the strongest pull of power. It's ancient."

Dean grabbed my hand in his. "There have been Meds who have figured out a way to siphon that ability, into a way of gaining access to its magic. And the only way they do that is by their self-made medication. It multiplies the blood cells in your body,--that's why you get sick and weak--allowing them to draw your blood. Then they separate the plasma from that blood and mold that into a gel. It's administered to the body in different ways, but it does all the same. Those who can't connect with the temple can now see it in their dreams, walking around ancient soil with the power of others swarming them."

"How do you know about the dreamscape?"

Callie widened her eyes. "So it's true."

Dean ignored her. "Yes. But it's not because of the treatments that the Med did when I was unconscious. I've always been able to go there. But I thought I was the only one who could do that."

So *did* I.

I guess there was no denying it now. That place--the dreamscape--was real. The people that were in there, *real*.

"But," I question, "This doesn't help explain anything? Why couldn't you find a file on Eric. Why are there a lot of people who don't have files on them? What's gonna happen to me when I get transferred to the capital. Will I be an experiment? A blood bag, easy for the pickings? I can't accept that."

That would make sense why Alice and the others live in that jungle/forest area. Is there a way I can join them? Is it even safe there? The last time I was there, I remember an arrow flying passed me. It hit Alice in the shoulder. She was bleeding. A lot.

She acted like it was nothing.

"He's like me." Dean pulled me from my thoughts.

"What do you mean? I thought you were like me? You have abilities too, don't you?"

"Yes. But I'm different. Eric and I are known as Anchors.

That's what people call others who can transfer or deflect someone else's magic."

"I'm confused. You're saying you can use my powers against others? How's that possible?"

He shrugged. "How do you have powers?"

I didn't really know. "So," my brow scrunched, "Does that mean you can also use my powers against me too?"

"That and take them away. That's why we're called Anchors. We can stop you from getting out of control. We can anchor you."

My shoulders tensed. "Then why hasn't he stopped me before?"

Does he want me to use them? Exhaust me?

Callie shrugged. "Maybe he doesn't know how to use his abilities."

Or he doesn't know that he has them.

"Either way," Dean added under his breath, "An Anchor has to have a strong tie to you. A bond if you will. And it has to be a strong one."

Like,

Friendship

I look up at Dean. "That's seriously cool."

Callie looked between us, confused. Then she rolled her eyes. "Dean told me about this. You're doing that telepathic speech thing, aren't you?"

I nodded. I finally felt like I wasn't going crazy. I really was able to hear other peoples voices in my head.

"But only those with a magical ability can do that. And even then you have to have some sort of bond with them to hear them. Other than that, nothing happens."

There was a knock at the door. Brooks popped his head in. He saw me first.

I'd almost forgotten that I was here for a dinner party. With--

"Dinner's ready. And the guest of honor is awaiting your presence promptly."

"So proper," Callie whispered under her breath.

He leaves when I say "Thank you." And after, I'm standing,

Callie and Dean follow shortly behind.

But what did this mean about Alice? When I shared my memory of the transfer form with her, she unknowingly shared one with me as well. The memory of a face. The one of a handsome man.

I didn't recognize him.

We were already down the stairs, Callie leading the way into the dining room.

There was the man. The one in Alice's memory. It was uncanny. Charcoal hair, sharp blue eyes. A wicked smile.

"Well if it isn't the astounding trio." he looked at each of us as he said our names. "Dean Harrington. Callie Underwood." he paused on my name. "It's nice to finally meet you Ms. Wanda Cannon."

The air around the room became unsettling.

"It's nice to finally meet you as well, Blake."

My jaw was starting to tighten. I didn't like the feeling I was getting. It was as if he was feeding bad energy throughout the room with just a look.

"What's wrong? It looks like you've seen a ghost."

I force myself to relax beside Callie. I can feel Dean side-eyeing me. He had to feel what I was feeling, right? Surely so. I smile and shake my head. "Not so much a ghost, but--a familiar face. I've heard so much about you these last couple weeks."

"Oh?" I've peeked his interest, "Is that so? Please do tell me what people have told you. Surely it wasn't anything bad." his gaze shifted toward Dean when he said that. Then it was back on me, his feet inching forward as his words grew snake like. "I'd been itching to come here for several months now, but you know how it goes. Work always carries you away from things."

Underwood cleared his throat at the end of the table. It's as if he's trying to save me. "Please. Let us sit and eat before the food gets cold."

Blake's eyes never veer away from mine. "Of course. Let us eat."

030.

ONE STEP BACK

[CALLIE]

I'd been wrong from the start. I'd been so oblivious. Too preoccupied with my own desire to street fight--allowing myself to run away from my problems rather than facing them--then to actually notice that anything else was happening. Like the world changing. Like people actually getting hurt.

I knew all this information already, spun by the words of Dean months and months ago from conspiracies that I thought were just making him insane. But no, he'd been right from the beginning. I didn't want to believe any of it.

How foolish was I?

"It's nice to finally meet you as well, Blake."

Blake Blackburn.

Man what a tongue twister. This guy was renowned for his work. When Dean and I finally cracked the system for the

Database room, this was the first person Dean dug around for. Not a surprise that there wasn't much there--other than what you can find online if you have access to a Tela-pad. How much he's done for the King, by his side. All the press work he's done to help social interactions calm down. The many, many charities he's funded for good causes.

But there had been some subject forms for experiments he had done in secret.

And here of all things.

Not a lot--two to be exact--and there really wasn't much to go off of.

No IDs.

No names.

No pictures to identify if the subjects were even human or mythical.

Nothing.

Dean said it was the perfect connection. Meaning what he said about Meds creating the medication to suppress peoples' powers all came from one person in particular. The one who made it first.

Blake Blackburn. "I'd been itching to come here for several months now," he says, "but you know how it goes. Work always carries you away from things."

His eyes wouldn't leave Wanda's.

Uncle Shawn cleared his throat. By the look on his face, he was definitely irritated. "Please. Let us sit and eat before the food gets cold."

He always did love his food.

I help Dean to a seat across from me. Wanda sits next to me and my uncle. Blake sits across from her. Still, his eyes never veer away.

Not until I clear my throat. "Blake, was it?"

He nods to me.

"I must ask." From the corner of my eye, I can see Wanda is fidgeting with her hands under the table. "What is so exciting about your job?"

"Well," he smiled, "There are a lot of exciting things that happen when you're in my position. Being the right hand for the king can have its perks."

Like being the mad scientist to an evil villain?

"Please indulge me. Are the missions intense? Is the pay good? Do you get free things now that you're a celebrity in the societal eye?"

"Callie," Uncle Shawn snips, "That's enough."

Blake waves him off. "It's not too much to answer. She's curious. I like that." He was the last one to start shoveling food onto his plate. And unlike everyone else, he was piling it high. "Say," he scooped a big heap of mashed stuffing into his spoon, "Your uncle was telling me about those street fights you'd always get yourself into. What was the Bar called again? Delta, Lamda--something?"

He knew what he was doing. He knew what I was doing.

We were both pushing the other to get information. In the process, both of us would be watching. Watching in-waiting for the moment that one of us would slip up.

Clever.

"And what a story it was to hear about your most challenging competitor."

Ah, yes. In the ring, we went by street names. Titles.

"Crusher Cain. That's who you're thinking of."

"Yes, yes. And who would have thought that your most hated fighter was now your Guide. Cassidy Kane, was it?"

I rolled my eyes. Both their names stunk worse than the back alleyways of Omega Bar's building. Anyone homeless thought it was the perfect place to shit their problems away. Figuratively and literally.

When I agreed to fight my Uncle's most skilled fighter, I hadn't expected it to be Kane. I had thought it'd be the know-it-all book worm fighter, who plays by the rules. Maybe some rules would be overlooked for a fight with me, but not all of them. It was as if I forgot all that I knew in a moment when I saw him.

My body aches with the memory of it all.

Blake's eyes veered toward my uncle as I shoved my face full of food.

"The improvement is growing, yes?"

Uncle Shawn finished his tall glass of wine. "Of course. She's welcome to show you later if you like."

I almost choke on my food as I force it down.

There was a reason why he'd kept his position for this long. It's said that most ranking positions, even as high as his, were outlived after two or three years. But his--seven and a half years later--is record winning.

"I'd do it, but," I hide my fear with a wicked grin, "I wouldn't want to hurt your feelings."

He laughs. "You've got some spirit, I'll give you that."

I nod, looking to Dean for comfort. His smile is small, but enough to calm my nerves.

"What about you dear?" Blake looks at Wanda again. She tightens her jaw as if not to shake.

She swallows her food. Smiles. "It's going well. I can feel myself getting stronger by the day."

"That's good to hear. It seems your medication is doing wonders then."

I could feel the air around the room rise several degrees. Either that or I was blushing.

It had to be the first. I was looking between Dean and Wanda, and both their faces were growing pale. It almost looked as if they were speaking to each other through that telepathic speech thing again.

What were they thinking, I wondered.

I clear my throat again. Blake looks at me. "Why do you have people take that medication anyway?" I question, "I've heard that people die from taking it for too long."

"And where'd you hear that ridiculous information from?"

Wanda. She said her guide's mother died from it. She said he thought it was her powers that did it. Not the medication.

Now his little sister was taking it.

"I've read news articles."

He shakes his head. "You can't believe everything you read or see. Most of that is just hogwash if you ask me."

"So, are you saying that everything about 'Alice and her Renegades' is just a tall tale?"

His eyes sharpened at the title.

Wanda's frame stiffened as well.

"What do you really know about them?" Blake prodded.

I was treading dangerous waters. Better his eyes on me than on Wanda, am I right? Seeing as he probably doesn't know about her quitting, means that Wanda's guide--Eric--hasn't put it in his reports. And seeing how he treats her when I look at them, he's willing to put his job on the line to protect her.

I'd have to thank him for that later.

"I know enough to see that you're the real villain here. Using other people's powers for your own selfish needs is pretty low if you ask me. Even for the King. It makes sense why he sends you instead. He can't handle the truth."

"Which is what?"

"That what you're doing for your selfish motives isn't really helping our country at all. All you do is lie, and lie, and--,"

"That's enough!" Uncle Shawn snaps. "You're making a fool of yourself."

Wanda stands fast from her chair. Then I notice the tight breeze whipping around the room. "I need air." She grabs my arm. "Callie, please take me outside for some air."

Blake stands, says, "I can do that," and I'm shaking my head, standing as well.

"We've both had enough to say. I'm excusing ourselves for the time being." I wrap my hand around Wanda's waist as we turn for the entrance. Her eyes are closed tightly, breathing heavy breaths. Whispering to herself as we leave, closing the door behind us. Brooks is there to stop us.

"Where are you taking her?"

I hold out my hand to stop him from touching her. "Give her space. She's having a panic attack."

He steps back. I walk her down the steps to the concrete path. Then we both slumped down to the grass.

She sighs.

"Better?"

She nods. "Yeah."

Her eyes were still closed.

"What happened back there?"

"What did it look like?"

I shrugged. I didn't really know exactly. "It looked like you were about to pass out."

She laughed. "Close."

"Were you and Dean talking through that mind-to-speech thing?"

She shook her head, dipping it into my shoulder. "I don't know how to explain it. When I speak to him it's like speaking to him, just without moving my lips. Vice versa. But," there was a pause where she reached for her chest, fisting her uniform shirt tightly.

"But what?"

"I don't know. It was like there was something draining me in there. Just being in the room with that guy . . . I couldn't breathe."

"Can you breathe now?"

"Yeah," she nodded. "But, my body feels weird for some reason. Could you smell anything really sweet in there?"

I shook my head. I didn't know what she was talking about.

"What did it smell like?" I asked.

She didn't answer.

"Wanda?" I moved my shoulder to nudge her. Then she was slumping into my lap, unconscious. "Wanda!"

I shake her shoulders. Come on! Come on! Wake up!

I push my fingers into her neck. My heart drops to my stomach. Then I turn and stand. "Help! Help! Please! She needs help!"

Brooks is bounding down the stairs, sliding to a stop. "What happened?"

"She--I don't know. She just passed out. I don't know what happened."

He checks for her pulse again. "Her heart rate is slowing. I thought you said she was having a panic attack."

"She was! Is! Can you please help her already? I don't know what to do!"

He runs back inside. I'm rocking her back and forth. *Wanda. Oh, Wanda, please. Wake up! Wanda, please!* "Wake up, Wanda!"

Everyone is storming outside. Except,

"Uncle, where's Dean?"

He's grabbing my hand. Pulling me away. Blake is bending down beside her.

"Hey!" I try to pull away.

I need to stop him.

"What are you doing? Stop!"

Kane is grabbing my arms. Pulling me away.

Blake's pulling something out of his pocket. Brooks is blocking my view.

I try to break free. "Let me go! She needs help. Let me see her! Stop!"

I hear a gasp.

Brooks is pulling Wanda into his arms. There's something around her arm. She's looking around in a daze.

She's okay!

"Wanda!" I call out.

Blake looks at me. "Get her back inside."

"Wanda," I reach out, "Please!"

She's okay!

Kane is dragging me inside. Uncle Shawn is closing the

door behind him. I look into the dining room as we pass. Dean's slumped over the table. Unconscious.

Dean? What the hell was happening? "Dean!"

031

DEFLECTION

[ERIC]

Turns out there is a third way to get rid/stun someone's powers: DEATH (it's quite the obvious answer, but darker than I'd prefer to admit...)

From "My Thoughts / Mixed Studies"--SRP

My first stop was a little market out of my hometown of Milagin. In the richest part of town stood this corner shop catered to baked goods and sweets. Their most famous dessert was the Gelime cream cake; Sonia's favorite.

She'll love this!

I wave my thanks to the shop owner before getting back into my escort car. General Underwood was generous enough to lend a driver out of his own pocket so that I could get home faster.

I'd slept most of the night-drive here, then asked that we stop for Sonia's gift.

The last time I'd gotten a Gelime cake was for my departure before I left for boot camp.

It'd been so long ago . . .

I opened the door for Turner--the driver--and hauled in our bags before closing the door. "Just put them in the living room for now. I'll get them later."

He nodded and disappeared down the hall.

All the lights were out. No one was home. Good. Sonia must've been with Ms. Garner still.

I could set up my surprise.

No one had seen me pull into my driveway. Normally the kids around the block would be biking around. Playing games and getting into trouble. Not to mention on a day like this--the sun was out, a cool breeze blowing slowly across the street-- even the adults would be sitting outside. Everyone would be enjoying the calm weather.

I set the cake down onto the kitchen counter and peek out the front window. The whole street was empty.

Strange, I thought. Where was everyone at?

I knew a couple of neighbors across the street who had powers. Those were the people who stayed inside the most. They had their blinds closed most of the time, and their house was normally spick-span. I remember how no one even stepped foot on their property without a reason. But they were nice all the same.

"What's wrong?" Turner asked.

I pulled away and looked at him in the doorway again. "Nothing. Just seems odd that no one is outside."

He shrugged. Some strands of his long hair fell around his face. "They're probably staying warm inside. Did you check the weather?"

I shook my head. I was too preoccupied with the thought of seeing my sister again to even care about anything else.

He was pulling one more bag inside.

"Maybe I should go and see my sister now."

He shrugged. "You do you, man. I'm just here for the ride."

"You'll be fine here while I'm gone?"

"Yep."

"Okay." I step onto the porch. "I'll be down the street if you need me."

He gave me a thumbs up from down the hall. "See ya later!"

I close the door. Look around at the quiet houses. It seems so strange to be back home. It's nice.

I'd have to bring Wanda here sometime. I bet she'd love it here.

I shake my head. *No. I can't be thinking about her right now.* I pounce down the stone steps and start my path down to the Garner home. It sat right at the end of the street. It was the one house that trumped all others. But not only was it the biggest house on the block, but it was also the most cared for.

The whole Garner family was a group of fostered individuals. Ms. Garner was the keeper of the house. Her eldest daughter was one of Sonia's closest friends. Mr. Garner died years before Ms. Garner adopted her first daughter. Then after my family moved into our childhood home, Ms. Garner had adopted five more children. Two more girls and three boys.

How many had she adopted this time? Two? Five? Twenty? After several laws were passed for those who had powers, parents were abandoning their kids to the streets because the Relocation wasn't an option if it was the kid's fault.

I rolled my eyes. I wish there were more people like Ms. Garner. Sweet, Kind. Not prone to throwing kids onto the street for something they didn't mean to do. Or even mean to be.

I heaved a shaky breath as I knocked on her door. My body was numb with nerves of excitement. *How tall was Sonia now? How beautiful had she gotten? Did she look like mom?*

I heard footsteps and unconsciously wiped my shirt clear of dust. It needed to be straight.

Then I noticed the dead flowers sitting by her door. It cracked open. "Yes?"

"Ms. Garner? It's me, Eric."

The door opened wider. Her wrinkled skin was paler. Her eyes sucked of all their life. "Eric?"

"Sonia said she was still with you." her eyes widened. "Is she here?"

She shook her head.

My eyes scrunched. "Is she with Sarah?"

"She's gone."

"Gone where?"

"They took her."

I looked behind me. She was staring into space. "Ms. Garner, are you okay? Have you taken your medicine?"

By the way she looked, she could be in her late eighties. But she never spoke her age. Who knew if she was almost eighty or ninety?

She shook her head. "They took them. All of them."

"Who took who?" My heart was cracking. There were needles pricking my skin all over. "Where is everyone?"

I look past her. No kids ran down her halls. *Where were all the toys?*

"They took them."

I look back to our street. No one was outside. Every lawn was filled with dead grass.

This wasn't strange. This was the Relocation.

"Ms. Garner." I turned my eyes sternly on her. "You need to tell me everything. Now."

Her eyes finally met mine. Tears pooled down her skin. "She's gone, Eric. They buried her yesterday."

“Who?”

“Sonia.” she sobbed. “They buried Sonia!”

032

IN BETWEEN NOWHERE

[WANDA]

"Wanda, look at me! Please!" Gem was shouting, yelling at me as she stood in front of me. "Why won't you look at me!? What's wrong?!!"

I shook my head, cupping my ears, trying to block out all the noise around me. "Please! Gem, just go away!"

I remembered why I couldn't look at her; why I can't give in.

She was shouting the same thing over and over again. "Look at me! Look at me! Look at me!"

The wind I was protruding was blowing us back and forth— side to side. She was using her own power to hold me in, as mine tried to push her away. It was as if I was on a ship in a thunderous storm, the ship swaying side to side as it was about to flip over. I felt the cool touch of someone's hands on mine, and I could feel my body begin to shake. My power was becoming weak, my body exhausted from all the exertion.

"Wanda. Please calm yourself before you get hurt."

Alice.

She used her own power to pull through to me, using the ground to physically root me down. She used her hands to pull mine away, whispering into my ears slowly. "Take a deep breath. In and out like me, okay?" I followed her speed, taking in a deep breath, and holding it for a moment before releasing it in a slow decline. It allowed me to focus on one thing. To calm myself.

Alice kept repeating herself, allowing time for my mind to relax once again. She held my face in her hands and I kept my eyes closed still. I couldn't risk giving her away. "Look at me. You're safe. We're safe. No one is going to hurt you. You can trust us. Just open your eyes, okay?"

I shook my head. "I can't. I-I ca-can't! They know! I can't stop them!" My voice was hoarse from screaming. From crying out for so long.

"What are you talking about? You're safe here. No one can enter here, except us. You're safe! Open your eyes!"

I pushed at her. Tried to escape her root hold on me. She held strong. "Please!" I pleaded with them. Begging them, "Let me go! Leave! I will not forgive myself if something were to happen to you! Please listen to me and go! GO!"

It was quiet. The only sound of my breathing and the wind whistling in my ears. Then I felt something envelop me and I felt the cold touch of Alice's hands again.

"Do you trust me?" She said, her roots releasing their hold on me and disappearing into the ground again.

I nod my head.

I felt I could trust her with my life.

"Then open your eyes, and look into mine. Do nothing else."

I hesitated for a moment. I wouldn't forgive myself. This is a real place. These are real people!

I try to focus.

If something were to happen to them . . . I'd never be able to live it down.

"Wanda, look at me. You'll be okay." She paused only for a moment before adding, "I'll be safe."

She cupped my face once again and I opened my eyes. I looked straight into hers and never dared to look away. Her eyes were glossy, watering with tears just like mine. I took deep breaths as she held me and as she closed her eyes, she rested her head on mine. She had thrown a blanket over us, shielding us from the world outside of it.

who is doing this to you? She asked.

I closed my eyes. She repeated her question.

who's doing this to you? who is--

"Blake--! Blake is doing this to us."

She looked at me puzzled. "Us? Who else is with you?"

I felt the tears pool down my face. They were warming my cheeks before they froze to my face, making my teeth grit. "My friends."

"What're their names?"

"Callie Underwood and Dean Harrington. They've been here with me."

She wiped the tears away from my eyes. "Where is here, Wanda? Where are you?"

"E—," I fell forward, reaching back with my hands to clutch the back of my skull. I felt the sharp pain of needles at the base of my neck. Crawling up to the crown of my head, stabbing as it went. I whimpered at the familiar pain. I sobbed into the ground, squeezing my eyes tightly shut.

I could hear Alice and Gem calling my name. "Wanda! What's wrong!"

I felt the electricity flow through every nerve in my body. I felt the heavyweight of the band wrapping around my left arm.

The same band that Blake used to pull me out of my dream, time, and time again.

I reached out to pull it off, but it wasn't there. It never is. Not here.

"WANDA!"

I looked up, the jungle swarming around us. I yelled for them to leave. To run and never turn back. All they did was stand frozen, staring at me with terror in their eyes. I could only imagine what they were seeing.

Me, on the ground, flickering in and out of visibility right in front of their eyes. A lightbulb in a pitch-black room, only visible when on, and gone when out. I could only fight for so long before I surrendered, leaving the room to be flooded with darkness.

I hear murmurs, non-familiar. I flutter my eyes open and

turn my head to the side. I was hoping to be alone. I wasn't.

Blackburn was at my side leaning in to see my face up close. He was expressionless. He was checking my eyes with a small light. "Well done, dear."

I cleared my dry throat. It was still hoarse from screaming for so long. "Please stop."

He searched my face as I stared at him.

He stepped back a few steps. "Why should I? You've been working with them."

I shook my head. My heart was racing. Tears were pricking my eyes as I fought them back. "You were forcing them to do things they didn't want to do! Like you're doing now--to me." I coughed. I was drenched in sweat, my cheeks flaring with the immense heat.

I saw his jaw tighten, grinding his teeth side to side. I finished my words. "Lucky for them, they were able to escape. I've told you. You'll never find them."

He snickered, his face morphing to fit a devilish smile. "Sooner or later, you will show me. I can promise you that, dear."

I mustered my strength and spit in his face. "Go to hell."

He wiped his cheek and turned to the door. I was still chained down, blankets strapped over me. The heat was making my body numb. It made me sleepy.

My eyes were growing heavy again. "Please," I pleaded. "Just let me go."

Blake was at my door. Stopped for a moment as if he was about to turn and say something, then he opened the door, and left.

033

THE RIGHT FOOT HOLD

[ALICE]

Time was slipping away.

"You went where?!" Leah yelled.

. . . And we were all hitting a dead end.

"I needed to go, Leah. You know we couldn't wait any longer." I'd gone to Hightown without her. And to the very lab that they had held us for experimenting only a year ago. She was huffing at me. Angry. "You saw her! She's weak. He's killing her!"

"That hadn't bothered you before."

I roll my eyes. She was right. "But aren't you tired of hiding?"

She looked at me, her nostrils flaring.

"You know I'm right," my hands fisted. "People are dying.

Kids are dying."

She opened her mouth. Closed it.

"I saw them, El. I saw what they were doing to them." I clenched my jaw. Pinched my eyes shut. I didn't want to think about them again.

"It's okay," she cupped my face, "We all thought it'd end with us."

"But it didn't. The King signed more laws. Blake got his lab rats."

"But he doesn't have us." I opened my eyes. Her gaze was seiring my irises. "That's what matters."

"All those people, El."

She shook her head, resting our foreheads together. **Listen,** her inner voice was speaking. **We fight for our people. We save those who fight for us.**

I shook my head. **Not anymore.**

We fight for our people. We save our people.

Leah pushed us apart. "And you trust she's worth saving?"

"If we fight against the current, we'd drown in the shallows."

She folded her arms. "Then what's your plan? We still don't know where she is."

I shook my head. "Not entirely."

Her eyes widened. "You found her location? How'd you do that?"

I pulled the key-card from my pocket. I'd snatched it from a Med when I was passing by a fight. I thought it was perfect timing that a soldier was threatening a nurse--if he didn't show him his sister, he'd find her himself. Strange guy. When I slipped into the corner of a hall--hoping not to get caught by passing guards--he said something that caught my attention.

He said: "Either you let me see her, or I call Blackburn myself! He'll have all your jobs!"

"He said that?" Leah questioned. "Who was that guy?"

I shrugged. I didn't know. Not until--

I found the data room. And when I searched Wanda in the system, the guy in the foyer was popping up next to hers.

Eric Florbal. Soldier to E-MATE Base. Also known as the

Environmental Maintenance Association of Trading Exports. A training base for new recruits, East of the Capital, and south of a small town called Cedarville.

That was hundreds of miles away.

His mother was part of the Marked. So was his sister.

"Did you find him afterward?"

I shook my head. "When I turned down the hall, guards were already dragging him away. I don't know where."

"Probably a temporary cell."

I nodded my head. They'll keep him there until someone comes to pick him up. Either that or release him in the morning.

A soldier like him--with his status--wouldn't stay there long.

"He's her Anchor."

Leah stared at me.

I scrunched my brows. "And I don't think he knows yet."

034

YOU'RE ALL THAT I HAVE

[ERIC]

The rest of the way back to base, Turner didn't speak to me. Didn't look at me.

Brooks was the one to help me out of the car, my restraints clanking.

"Take them off," Blackburn spoke, "He has no use for them anymore."

Brooks nodded and left with my restraints. Valmore's old office door closed behind him.

Files were sprawled out around the room. "Love what you did with the room," I commented.

He didn't care to acknowledge my words. "Care to indulge me on why you broke into one of my facilities?"

Ms. Garner said a couple of officers took the kids to a

facility in Hightown. The same building I was planning on taking my sister to be treated. Demanding answers only got me thrown into a holding cell.

I don't think I cried more in my life.

My sister was gone. *My sister was gone . . .*

I didn't want to believe it. I couldn't. Not without seeing it myself. I needed to see her. See the body for myself.

I shook my head, not wanting to look at him. I had believed that what Blake was doing was for the best of others. For those that were part of the Marked. I didn't know the extent of the damage. Of the Relocation.

He repeated his question. "Why did you do it?"

My nose was starting to burn again. "Why are you doing it?"

"Doing what?"

"You're gonna kill her. Aren't you? It's not the medication she should be weary of. It's you."

Silence followed for a long moment. "You're talking about Ms. Cannon now?"

I needed to think of the present. Think of Wanda.

She needs me. I can feel it.

"Why are you testing on her?" I look up. "You're gonna kill her if you don't stop."

Brooks had filled me in while he was walking me here. Told me Blake was trying to get into a dreamscape that Wanda had access to.

That must've been where she'd gone in her dreams--so many times before, I'd thought.

He rolled his eyes. "I can't trust any men around here, can I?" He pulled his hands back behind him. "Do you know why I let you come back?"

"Because you can't find any more orphans to boost your ego?" I jab.

He laughs. Shakes his head. "No."

"Is it because you need your own therapist? Clearly you need the help--."

"Have you heard of an Anchor?" He cut me off. He looks at me. Dead on.

My jaw tightens. I shake my head.

He smiled. "An Anchor is someone who grounds another. Either by emotional, physical, or mental bonds, Anchors can manipulate their other half by using their powers against themselves. Ms. Cannon's friend--Harrington, I believe--is one."

"But he doesn't have powers."

"That you know of. Anchors can't prove their magical. They can only do that by bonds. Trials and other means to test it. You--are one of them."

"What are you talking about? That sounds delusional."

I'd never heard of an Anchor before.

"Ah! But it's not. And you know I'm right."

I held back for a moment. This man wasn't just hurting Wanda as we spoke here, he was reveling in it. He was wasting my time.

"You can't seriously be saying that the only reason why I'm still here is that I'm this Anchor you say I am. I'm the best of the best."

"Is that what Nick told you?"

He was talking about Valmore. The one person who said I was perfect for the job. Things were starting to click into place. Why I'd been given his position when he left. Why I was still Wanda's guide when that position wasn't mine anymore. All of the training with her, all of it.

"It was because of you."

He shook his head. "Not entirely. You helped with it just as much as I did. You made a connection with her. A bond. You became her Anchor."

"Stop putting things in my head."

"How did I know, when you were the last man to stand in the room before her, that you had feelings for her? That you cared for her more deeply than anyone could ever imagine?"

Petition day. He was the one who asked why I stayed so long.

He's wearing the same black uniform.

I shake my head. "You're delusional."

"Stop lying to yourself! It wasn't me who forced you to fall in love with her. You did that of your own desire."

I didn't want to admit it.

"Do you think I didn't know? I can see what she sees in you. What you see in her. You both love each other but can't because you're a soldier and she's an experiment. Don't you see how ridiculous that sounds? It sounds ridiculous!"

"You're crazy!"

"No, I'm smart. And I won't stop you from loving her. Do you know why?"

I stiffened my neck.

"The reason why is because by the end of this whole thing, she'll be the one who will kill you. Not the other way around."

I shook my head. "You're gonna kill her if you don't stop your tests. You need to stop this."

His eyes flared into a raging sea. "She's gotten to you." He scoffed. Shook his head with disbelief. "I can't believe it. I'm dealing with children."

He turned back from speaking to himself.

"If you don't want to take my orders, then factor this into that thin skull of yours. Either you do what you're told, or I, myself, pledge to plunge a knife into your back. Then you'll just be dead. And I'll continue my tests as I see fit. How does that sound? Reasonable enough for you?"

I tightened my jaw. I had nothing else to lose. He was more insane than I had thought. More gruesome. Heartless.

"I want to see her."

He tilted his head. "I'll be pausing her tests this evening to start with her friends. You can see her then. In the morning, I'm sending her to the capital."

I take a step forward. "She's too weak to travel. You need to give her time."

He shook his head. "Not unless you give her this," he held out a vile.

Inside was a dark liquid. "What is it?"

He placed it in my hand. "It's called Damp Moss. Extracted from the richest forest of Sinitallious. It can put the subject into a very deep sleep. Almost like a coma, if you will."

I shake my head. "I'm not giving this to her. No way."

His facial expression darkened into something monstrous. "Either you do it," his jaw was tightening, "or I do it. Your call."

I clench my hand around the vile. I didn't like this. "I'll do it." I didn't like this at all.

"Good. Then you'll be on the next trip to the capital."

"When will I see her again?"

"In three days time. Then she's all yours."

035

HOLD ME TIGHTER

[WANDA]

The room was shrouded in darkness. I couldn't keep track of the time. A Med must've turned out the light while I was asleep.

I tried to pull myself loose from my restraints. I gave up, frustrated. Still, no budge.

Then, I heard the muffled sounds of feet outside my door, and I called out to them. "PLEASE! SOMEONE LET ME OUT OF HERE!"

The door opened after a moment, and I felt my heart melt to the floor. Eric rushed to my side looking at the damage. He pulled at the belts, flinging the blankets to the ground. Then he ripped the cuffs loose, throwing them out to the floor as well.

Next thing I know, he's pulling my frail body into his arms. Dipping his head into the nape of my neck, he whispered, "I'm so glad to see you're okay."

The cool air around us made me shiver. I pulled my body closer into his to keep his warmth. It wasn't like the sweltering heat, but it was enough to soothe my aching chest. I never thought I could miss his touch so much.

"It's been so long," I began to sob. "I felt so alone."

He smoothed down parts of my tangled hair. "It's alright. I'm here now."

I shake my head, allowing my cheeks to flood with tears. "No. You don't understand! I felt so alone. I was trapped in myself for so long. I felt like I couldn't breathe."

He pulls us apart. Questioning was in his eyes. "Can you breathe better now?"

I gave a weak smile. "Now that you're here."

He shakes his head, dipping it down. "I should have been here sooner. I would've stopped this at the beginning."

"But you didn't know."

"No I didn't. And I should've. I should've been here."

"Nothing would have changed. Blake has me under watch twenty-four hours a day. Nothing goes without him knowing."

"I know. I spoke to him."

My grip on his shirt tightened. "What did he say?"

"Nothing I shouldn't have already known by now."

"But--,"

"All that matters at the moment is that I can be here with you. He's allowed me this time with you for the time being, and I don't want to waste it."

My eyes furrow. *What had happened between him and Blackburn? What had he found out?*

"Then let's not waste it."

I pat the side of the bed and we dip into the mattress together. He pulls me closer, my head resting on his chest, and his head resting in my hair. I let out a small laugh. "Ya know, the whole time that you've been away, I don't think I've actually slept."

"Having bad dreams again?" he joked.

"You could say that." Closing my eyes I smile. "I'm glad I got to know you."

"Why's that?" he sighs.

"Because. You're the one person that I think truly gets me. Even more than my friends."

"Does that make me your *best* friend now?"

I yawn, "I suppose it does. But I can't deny that I'd rather you be more of a friend than anything else."

I felt my mind was slowing.

Eyes drooping down, darkness was enveloping me calmly. Eric's body shifted closer to mine and I sighed with comfort that he was here with me. If I could hold onto this feeling for a moment longer . . .

036

NOT MY FRIEND NO MORE

[CALLIE]

I could tell you I'd improved in my fighting skills, but up against Kane, there was no chance of success. He always seemed to have the upper hand.

Always.

I'd stressed every muscle in my body trying to get past him, but I never got past the first step off the porch. But not only did I stress every muscle. I'd stressed every option for escape.

There was no way I was going to get to see Wanda or Dean anytime soon. And Kane was making sure of that.

I sighed, dropping my arms to my sides. "I give up." I straightened my stance as best as my back could go and turned for the stairs. "There's no use."

I'd been at this fight for six days straight. Today was the

last straw.

"Where do you think you're goin'?" Kane hollered.

I pulled myself up the stairs waving my hand at him. "I need sleep. And a shower."

"You're giving up so easily?"

"There's no use, Kane. You've proven your point."

I can't, and wouldn't ever get out of this house without permission from my uncle.

I groaned, turning on the hot water. This blows. I was useless. I couldn't help Wanda when she needed me the most. I couldn't help Dean when he got stabbed. I couldn't help either of them, and I was trapped in this house--doing absolutely nothing--until Uncle Shawn said it was fine for me to leave.

Even then, he has his limits.

"Only to the library and back." He'd say.

"Once training is done, you come straight home." He'd demand.

I rolled my eyes. This was useless. How was I supposed to save my friends if I couldn't get past one measly little guard?

"Callie!" I heard my uncle holler.

I rolled myself onto the floor, my arms too loose to really hold my frame more than a couple inches from the ground.

Everything hurts.

"Callie!" He yelled again.

Once I was up, I swung the door ajar. "Alright, alright! I heard you the first time!"

I rubbed at my eyes as I slumped down the stairs.

"What is it? I was sleeping--,"

In the doorway, stood Dean. Nothing else seemed to matter. I ignored the Base uniform he was wearing. I ignored the fresh haircut.

"Dean--!"

Now I was flat on my back, a bag thrown into my abdomen.

What the hell . . . ? Did Dean just kick my feet out from under me?

"Callie," Uncle Shawn said, "This is Dean Harrington. Your

assistant guide."

I looked up at him confused. Looked at Kane then, as he snickered down at me.

What the actual hell was happening? "Dean?" I sat up. "What's going on?"

Uncle Shawn helped me up to my feet as I wiped the dust off my sweats. "Blake made some new advancements." He pointed toward Dean, who picked up the bag from the floor, shaking Kane's hand with a smile. "And Dean here is his first trial run."

Trial run for what?

Dean finally turned back to me, his eyes filled with curiosity. "You'll have to understand I did that for your own good."

"Kicking me onto my back and slamming your bag into my stomach? That was for my own good?"

He nodded, looking at my uncle. "Your uncle told me you can be a disaster waiting to happen if not treated right away."

Disaster?

Blake must've wiped his memory or something.

The thought made my heart drop to my feet. "My uncle told you that, did he?" I pulled myself away from the three of them. Clenched my hands as I did. "Did he also tell you you used to be my boyfriend?"

He shook his head. "I think I'd remember a pretty face like yours if I saw it."

My cheeks flush and drain of its color all at once. "Uncle," I snap, "What the hell did you do? Dean's mind is completely wiped."

"I didn't do anything."

"Bullshit," I take three quick strides forward. Dean puts himself in between us. "Get out of my way Dean!"

He shook his head. "You need to calm down."

"Or what?"

"Or I'll make you calm down."

I tightened my jaw. "I'd like to see you--,"

My neck was in his arm before I knew it. I hadn't thought he had it in him to grab me into a choke hold. But then again, I wasn't thinking that he was actually brainwashed.

Dean!

He dropped me before my vision blurred, and I heaved deep breaths off the floor. "Is that proof enough for you, Ms. Underwood?" he paraded.

I couldn't stand to look at him.

I heard Kane chuckle behind him. "This is gonna be fun."

PART TWO

LOCATION: HERIVERA, SINITALLIOUS

SEASON: WINTER

YEAR: 2203

037

NEWBIE

[ERIC]

I fold my arms. "Why is he here?"

Wanda's friend Callie stands next to Blackburn, who waves my attention toward Harrington again.

"I could say the same for you, pretty boy," Callie chimed. She was matching my posture.

Stiff. Tense.

"The transfer of Ms. Cannon was a success, thank you." Blakeburn nods. "I couldn't have done it without you."

"What's the move now? Am I supposed to babysit them too? I thought that was Kane's job."

"Actually it's *all* our jobs now," Harrington piped in.

Something wasn't right. He was different. And not just

because he was in a base uniform and had full gear on his belt. Callie wasn't keen on him either. Not like she was the last time I saw her. She was worried for him. For Wanda and him.

Did the tables just turn?

"Like I can handle more idiots in my line of work," I add.

"You'll help Dean here with the details. He'll be assisting Kane here shortly and he needs to understand the ropes of being a guide." He waves my disapproval away. "It's not like being both an Anchor and a guide can be that hard."

"Then why not get Kane to do it?"

Callie rolls her eyes. "And you think I haven't told him this already?"

"Enough," he snaps at her, "The reason why Eric is helping Dean is that they can help each other. They both are Anchors. They both have people to anchor to." his gaze shifted toward me, "He will help Dean. No questions asked. Correct?"

He promised to keep clear of Wanda if I followed his orders. It's his leverage over me, it seems.

I nod stiffly. "Of course. What would I rather be doing than helping out my commanding officer?"

Callie takes a step closer. "Please," she pleads, "they're delusional. My uncle won't tell me where he's put Wanda. She needs to be safe. Please tell me she's safe."

I look between her and Blake. Harrington is reaching to grab for her arm. I grab her myself and cut him off, blocking both Blake and Dean from her. She grabs the clearance card I've slipped to the back of my belt--just for her. I watch as she folds her arms in an attempt to cover-up what she's got.

"Forcing her isn't going to help," I snap at Harrington, "She's a person too. Respect her space when there's space to give."

He smiles. "It might work for you--sugaring the path for that Cannon girl--but it won't work on this one."

Cannon girl? He couldn't remember a damn thing, could he?

Blake backs up to clear the room. The smile shifted on his face slowly. He won't stop us from fighting this out, but he won't let anyone walk away.

I sigh. "Just because Cannon didn't care to fight me, doesn't mean she wanted to. It's not your job to push them around. It's your job to watch them. Act on their impulses and work on your feet."

He shifts to the side, reaching for Callie's arm. I swat him away. He shoves at my torso and I have to grab his arm, twisting it until he's leaning over, unable to move.

"And most importantly," I add, "You have to protect the one you're guiding."

"Who told you that one?" he winced.

"No one. It's just called being a good person. A good leader."

Then I push him forward. Blake catches him at his shoulders. Wipes his sleeves off. "I think it's best that we give you some time alone," he motions to Callie, "Callie, dear. Come along."

She looks up at me. Gives me the same look that Wanda does when she doesn't want to go somewhere. Callie's face is more fearful.

I nod, and she huffs out a sigh. Gives Harrington one last look before walking out of the room with Blake next to her.

"Now it's time for a real fight. Don't you think?"

I flex my jaw. "Do your worst."

Blake didn't seem to get the hint that I wanted to be left alone. Either that or he knew and just didn't care.

"Just tell me what you'll do to me now. I am the last one, aren't I?" I sigh. Finally, we made it back to the house, Uncle Shawn waiting for me outside. Thank god! I'd never felt more thankful to see him in my life. "My uncle tells me you tested something new on Dean. And seeing how he's lost his mind, can I at least know if I'm next?"

We pause in the middle of the path. The house is only a couple of meters away.

"Do you think I'd really do that to a lady?"

I snicker. "If you think of me as anything more than a lady then you're insane."

"But you are more than a lady. You're something special."

His words make my stomach knot with discomfort. "You flatter yourself. But cut the crap. Obviously, you're the man who knows the real reason I was brought back here. I saw it in my file. You signed the guardian certification. My uncle isn't really in full custody of me, is he?"

I'd figured it out the moment Blake arrived. Dean had passed out, and Wanda was disappearing down the path--back to the place she'd rather have died in. Blake had the power over my uncle. Enough to be in higher ranks than anyone here.

Superiority, that was an obvious thing. But to understand that being here, I was more valued caged, than out in normal society.

My curiosity was spiked.

"I have powers too, don't I?"

He smiled. "A quick one, you are."

I roll my eyes. "Then why can't I use them?"

His eyes narrowed. "It's a funny thing, magic. It's unpredictable. And dangerous."

"Like I'm not dangerous without them? I've lived this long without knowing. I've fought men with my bare hands. You don't think that's dangerous too?"

"It's ruthless, yes. But someone with powers, who can't use them, is an unstable powder bomb just waiting to blow."

I sneer. "And that terrifies you, doesn't it?"

He shakes his head. "Not at all."

He starts walking again. "Then what *does* scare you?" I ask.

"Nothing."

Blake finally left after lunch, saying he was heading back to the capital.

To Wanda, I think. Wanda's there. Alone.

I still grasp Eric's key card in my hand. Uncle Shawn is leaving for a meeting soon, and Kane and the others will be back to check on me. So I sit at my window waiting.

waiting

waiting . . .

"Underwood!" I hear Dean shout. I stand quickly and hide behind the door. Waiting is the best game to play for this. "Underwood!" he calls again, his voice moving closer.

Almost there.

Almost--

His foot reaches my door. He pushes the door slowly as he creeps closer.

There!

I slam the door into his body. I hear his head hit the door frame. Then the loud thud of his body hitting the ground stiffens my senses. I wait a few moments to hear if anyone else comes up.

Nothing.

I make my escape. If I can get to the Grand Hall, then I could hide out until dark to secure a better cover from all the patrols. Figuring in that Uncle Shawn would have soldiers looking for me, I'd need the extra cover.

Sprinting down the stairs, I'm skipping three at a time. Then I'm at the front door. I'm looking around the house to watch my back. Running down the path, quick on the balls of my feet, making fast work up to the Grand Hall. Then I pause.

Dean would look here first wouldn't he? Even though he doesn't have his memories, I'd bet you money that would be his first hunch. And he wouldn't even know why.

This was the first place we snuck out to. It was the night that Dean got wounded. We hid out here, knowing this would be the last place patrols would look. Then we made it to the entrance center without trouble.

Now--this is a different story.

Would he bring backup?

I shake my head. This new Dean thinks he's all that! He'd come alone to prove it.

Plan B then.

Eric's card got me into the back entrance of the gate building. In the garage, cars lined the side walls.

If only I had keys . . .

I hid in the shadows while I ran up the slope to the service gate. There was a guard on desk duty. Another watching the road outside.

I'm so close!

Once I get out, I can slip into the shadows. I can get help. Go to wherever Blake has Wanda and save her. Dean is for another day. He's not the one who's in trouble right now.

Wanda needs me.

I slip behind a car when I hear someone pulling up to the gate. The car blocks the gate soldiers and I can't hear what they are chatting about.

I hope no one sees me. I need to blend in.

Blend in . . .

One of them laughs.

I close my eyes. No one sees me. No one can hear me. But why does it feel like they can?

My chest tightens at the thought.

Wanda!

All I want to do is reach out like Dean does to Wanda. I want to reach my voice out and tell her, I'm coming for you. I'm coming!

WANDA!

There you are.

I feel my heart stop. Look around cautiously. The gate is clear, the car gone.

261

I could've sworn I heard Dean!

Dean?

The voice was so gentle. Like Dean was back to himself. I turn to the shadows again. I can't do this. Not without Dean. Not without--

There--

I pause.

There--

I found you.

My heart pounds. I can't breathe.

Dean?

His hand waves. My face drains. *Why can't I move?*

Something sharp hits the back of my head.

I gasp, *DEAN!*

039

IT'S NEW EVERYTHING

[WANDA]

A woman was shoving a cup of water in my face, demanding me to drink. I shook my head and pushed it away. *This isn't what I thought I'd wake up to.*

Her voice was filled with disapproval. "If you do not drink it, you cannot blame me if you faint."

I gave her a questioning look. "And who are you?"

Her words came out so casually. "Your maid."

Maid?

I must've been delusional. I wasn't in my hospital room anymore. Not even remotely close. I was laying in a large bed fit for four people. The corner posts blocking the mattress in a cube shape with drapes tied to each stilt.

Blake really out did himself now.

Beyond the bed, the room was ginormous. A fireplace stood at the end of the room. One chair on either side of a couch to fit the whole package. There's a door to the right by one of the four windows on the adjacent wall. The shear curtains holding little of the light from coming in.

She shoved the cup back into my space. "Now, drink."

I forced it back again. "Where am I?" On the wall behind the woman—the maid, as she called herself—was a set of double doors and at the center between the adjacent walls was another set of double doors.

The woman smiled and forced the cup into my hands. "You're at the King's private estate, dear. In the capital."

I felt my face drain of color. My heart lurched. The last thing I could remember was laying with Eric in my bed. "What's wrong, dear? You're growing paler by the minute?" She pushed my hands up to place the cup at my lips. "You really should drink some water."

I shoved her back hard. "Enough with the water! I don't want it!" I threw it toward the fireplace. The piercing shatter of glass on hardwood echoing as the only sound in the room.

The maid stumbled back.

I vaguely remember Blake telling me about this several

days prior. Something about my transfer coming up sooner than expected--due to certain circumstances.

"Where the hell am I?!"

"I just told you, miss. You're at the—"

"No!" I fisted the comforter and flung the mess of sheets back. Slung my feet over the side and stood slowly. The maid moved to grab me and I glared at her. "Don't! I got it."

"But—," she was unable to choose between doing her job or leaving me alone, "You shouldn't rush yourself, miss!" She pleaded.

This couldn't possibly be happening! I wanted to go home; not farther away!

I curled my toes on the cool hardwood floor before taking a deep breath. I need a new plan to escape.

"Why won't you let me help you, dear?"

"Because," I snapped. "I don't need your help. I need answers." I walked up and opened the closest doors. I was met by a swarm of dresses. A closet. *Wrong doors.*

I turned to the center doors. Those must be it. I flung the double doors open and smiled. Yes!

I stepped into the large hallway and looked side to side.

"What do you think you're doing?" Blake took leisure strides toward me, his pride hanging over him like a gold medal. "Who let you out, dear?"

Both of us turned to the maid scurrying out. She seemed scared and her shoulders hunched as she spoke to Blake's feet. "Please forgive me, Lord, sir. She was going to hurt me again if I didn't stop her. She wouldn't stop!"

I gaped at her, stunned. Blake looked at me the whole time. I closed my mouth after a moment and tightened my jaw. There wasn't going to be any way of escaping this.

"Thank you, Ms. Fitzgibbons."

She nodded her head and bowed before scurrying away down the hall. I watched her turn the corner and disappear. I held my ground when Blake eased himself into my space. He didn't say a word, but rather bent down to my eye level.

He smiled.

"Why am I here?" I growled.

He cupped the side of my face and I flinched out of the way. All he did was move even closer. "I know we've already had this conversation, Wanda."

I kept stepping back, trying to make space between us. I stopped when my legs bumped the back of the couch and I looked back to catch myself. Blake grabbed the back of my neck in a moment and pulled my face close to his.

"It's just you and me, dear. There's no need to hide yourself from me now." He pulled me closer and closer.

I spit in his face. When he flinched away I slapped him across the face. Hard. "Get the hell away from me!"

He opened his jaw to pop it back into place. Looking at something beyond the doorway he spoke. "If I catch you doing something you're not supposed to do, I'll personally punish you."

I swallowed hard and cleared my throat. I tried not to sound so scared. "And what am I supposed to do?" *Sit here like a pretty doll and play dress up?* I'd break his jaw before I do that.

That's when he looked at me. Dead on, and no emotion clear. "Read a book, sit, eat, and bathe." *He couldn't be serious?!* "Under no circumstances are you allowed out of your chambers without me or your guide."

I opened my mouth to interject but he held up his hand. "Don't speak until I'm done." I closed my mouth and bit into my cheek. He continued. "Your maid will bring you meals and she will dress you, bathe you, and whatever else she must do. If I hear another complaint from her that you didn't do what she asked, I'll come and do whatever you wouldn't let her do myself."

He shifted only a step forward and I rushed to move around the couch to put ten feet between us. He didn't move any closer.

"Got it?"

I nodded my head. "Yeah, I got it."

He turned to the doors. "Good." I watched as he grabbed the handles. "Oh!" My eyes met his again, "and, if you break another glass, I'll break your hand."

My face paled faster than I could look over to the mess still left on the floor behind the couch. Water was in a puddle of sharp glass. I almost didn't want to look back as I nodded.

Then the door closed, no click of a lock needed. I was already trapped in my own body. Trapped in a place I had no clue of the direction. I had no mental map of this place. Of the city or town that I was in.

I was seriously screwed.

040

FEELING THE MOTION

[WANDA]

The Next Morning, I didn't have a single dream. Not one with magical places or people. Like me, I think. I'm alone here. But not so much anymore.

There are more people like me! Somewhere out there . . .

The maid--Ms. Fitzgibbons--brought me breakfast at six o'clock.

"How do you know the time?" I asked, stuffing a piece of fruit in my mouth. "I don't see a clock anywhere?"

She was undoing the making of my bed. Then she was doing it again. "You know it's improper to speak with your mouth full, dear."

I swallowed the piece of fruit. "Sorry,"

"Don't apologize. Just don't do it again."

I turned back to my plate. Poked at the scrambled eggs with my fork before deciding not to eat anymore. I still had a full plate, and now none of it seemed good in my eyes. I stood and walked up to the corner window by my bed. I sat in the indented sill and dipped my head into the glass. It was cold to the touch.

I didn't realize how fast winter would come. The snow here is already starting to fall.

How long has it been since I've seen a real snowfall? Has it really been ten years?

"The last time I saw snow was when I was seven."

"Do what--?" I turned to see Ms. Fitzgibbons in the connected bathroom. She came out, her face contorted. "Did you say something, dear?"

I hesitated on telling her. *Could I trust her?* "Nothing." I shake my head. She waits a long moment before turning back to her work.

I looked back outside. The street was filled with few people. Most of them were crossing down and up the street. Covered with fur coats and thick jackets.

The women had capes draped over their shoulders. Hoods that all of them had up to protect their beautiful hair. The men had either top-hats or bowler hats. Thick black coats and puffy scarves to keep them warm.

I pulled my legs closer to my chest. Watching them alone was making my body ache from the cold outside. It was enough to make me shiver.

Lunch came at twelve o'clock. "So," I looked at Ms. Fitzgibbons again. She hadn't answered my earlier question. "How do you tell the time around here?" I took a spoonful of the warm soup. I hummed with delight. It tasted of mushrooms, chicken, and carrots. A ting of salt left my mouth wanting more.

Ms. Fitzgibbons pulled something out from under her shirt. On a thin chain necklace hung a tiny digital-faced watch. The white numbers read 12:03 pm. *Oh.*

That's cool. "Do all the staff carry one?" I took another spoonful of broth, swallowing, "I mean, assuming that you aren't the only one here besides Blake. Surely there must be others."

She pushed the watch back under her shirt. Cleared her throat before turning to the doors. "I'll be back later to pick up your leftovers. I would advise you to finish eating everything this time." She was avoiding my questions again.

I shook my head.

"Can you at least answer one of my questions?"

She grabbed the door handles. "Yes." Then she was opening them and closing them behind her without another word.

Damn. That was a question!

I hadn't realized it was getting late until Ms. Fitzgibbons came back with dinner. She had come earlier to pick up my empty plate and bowl, but I really didn't bother to look. My eyes were focused on the world outside my window.

At the hospital, the only window I had was the one looking out into the hall. I knew hospitals had rooms like that, but the blinds were never shut. Mine were. I didn't like how people could easily peek in whenever they wanted. I felt I had no privacy.

I looked around the room again. Could there be a surveillance camera somewhere?

"What are you doing dear?" Ms. Fitsgibbons poked.

I turned to her for a moment before looking back. "Nothing."

I heard her feet move closer to me. I could feel her prying eyes on me. She leaned her head in my view and I turned to face her again. "Why do you keep looking out there, dear? Are you waiting for someone?"

I went stone-faced, ignoring her question. "Have you ever left this place?"

"What?" She was taken aback. Shook her head. "Why would you ask that? Of course I've left this place!"

I rolled my eyes and looked back out the window. The snow was falling harder. It was difficult to see all the people move up and down the street. But one figure caught my eye. A man was rushing out of the estate, weaving around the stream of people walking the opposite direction.

Is that Blake?

That's Blake!

Where's he going?

"Ms. Cannon. Ms. Cannon!"

I pulled back. "What?" I scrunched my brow and gave Ms. Fitzgibbons a mean look. "I was only—," her face was more wrinkled than ever. Yesterday I saw her as possibly being in her early forties, but she looked more in her fifties now. I could spot the gray strands of hair pulled into her low bun.

Her eyes were more sunken in and harsh as she questioned, "Why would you ask a rude question. It's not nice to mock status into someone's face."

"I wasn't trying to do that! I only asked because I've never gotten out on my own!" Hot tears stung at my eyes and I hadn't realized that I'd been bottling up this emotion for so long. "I just wanted to know if you were like me! Trapped in a place you didn't like!"

I don't want you to be a bad person like Blake, I wanted to say.

Her expression shifted into something dark. She sunk into the space in front of me. She didn't have to say anything to speak to me.

I choked on a sob and heaved a shaky breath. I didn't know where I was. I didn't know if my friends were going to be here. I didn't know if I was ever going to see Eric again.

My heart felt empty all of a sudden. "When I was little, my mom never let me go outside alone. I was always shadowed by someone, either one of my parents or one of my friends." I exhaled a sarcastic laugh. "And even then my mom didn't want me leaving the *safety of home*," I said mockingly.

"Then I was taken away . . . slept in a coma for seven years and got stuck in another place. I couldn't go where I wanted and when I had a secret place that I could go to, that was taken away too." I glanced at the double doors. "Now I'm here, in a place I never asked to be. Never wanted to be." I choked on another sob before crushing my knees to my chest and hiding my face inside.

"*Sshhh!*" I felt her arms around me. I hiccuped when I tried to calm my breathing. "It's going to be okay, dear. *Shh, shh, shh.*"

Time slowed just for me as I calmed myself down. I didn't know how much time had passed but it was long enough for the sun to sink into the sky and let the night rise high.

I turned to Ms. Fitzgibbons as she unwrapped her arms and stood. "Are you hungry, dear?" She was walking to the table. "I'm sure the food has gone cold by now. I could go down and grab something fresh for you if you want?"

I shook my head. "No," rubbing my eyes with a yawn, "I'm not hungry."

She put the plate back down on the table. Turned to me with a warm smile. "Then why don't I give you a bath. I'll make sure the water is nice and toasty."

I gave a weak smile and said, "Okay."

She walked into the bathroom. Called out, "Your nightgown is in the middle drawer, dear!"

"Okay!"

I went to the closet and pulled the door open. The swarm of dresses were back and I had to push them back so I could see the drawers under the skirts. In the middle draw—as she said—was nightwear. All of them silk nightgowns. I pulled out the first one I saw—a pale salmon color. Then I grabbed underwear.

"Set them over here." Ms. Fitzgibbons pointed to a cushioned chair in the corner with a small window above it.

I had only stepped into the water for a couple seconds. "Can I have privacy? Take my own bath?"

It's as if she changed completely. Her expression softened and she gave a warm, sweet smile. "Of course. I'll be back to check on you in a while." She nodded and left the room, closing the door behind her. In a moment the tightness in my chest loosened and I sighed.

Once I pulled the covers up to my chin, I closed my eyes. Ms. Fitzgibbons was already turning out the lights when she whispered, "How was your bath dear?"

"Wonderful," I sighed, "and just what I needed to escape for a while."

"What do you mean by that, dear?"

I rolled onto my side. Dug my face into the soft pillow. I could feel myself slipping into a deep sleep. I didn't even care. I let it sweep me off my feet and fly me away.

Darkness followed.

041

MISSING

[WANDA]

I still couldn't believe what I saw. Or better yet, smell.

This morning I woke up to the smell of coffee. Fresh coffee. Ms. Fitzgibbons wasn't anywhere, and I was completely alone. I dropped six sugar cubes into the hot liquid and hummed at the delightful smell. It made my stomach feel all warm inside without even taking a sip.

The sun was rising when I decided to put two more sugar cubes into my drink. Then once I took a sip, my mouth watered for more. I cupped it in my hands as I cozied up to my corner seat at the window. *I'm definitely growing to love this spot.*

Knock, Knock!

Come in, I thought.

The door opened a moment later and I didn't care to turn my head to see who it was. It could only be one of two people.

My guess was . . .

"It's a nice morning isn't it?" Blake.

I still didn't turn to look. Nodded my head calmly. "Indeed it is." A yawn grew and tears filled the corners of my eyes. I blink them away before I take another sip of my drink.

"Did you sleep well, dear?"

That's when I look at him. Every time he calls me dear, I want to slap him across the face. Letting loose a weak smile, "Yeah, I did." I lied. Last night was something I couldn't get out of my mind.

I thought I was back in the jungle with Gemma and Alice, but then when I looked around, nothing moved. There was no wind, no sounds, no sign that the jungle was even alive. I couldn't feel any energy in the air. It was stale and made my chest feel as if I was being crushed under someone's foot. It felt like a normal dream. If that's what a dream felt like.

I couldn't feel anything when I was there. When I stuck my hand in the dirt and crushed the soil in my hand, letting it crumble grain by grain out of my hand, all I could do was watch it fall. I couldn't feel its touch or the cold press when I smashed it together.

Nothing.

I felt like I sat there all night before I drifted back into my body again. When I woke up, my body was completely numb. Only when I stood to grab the cup of coffee in my hand did my nerves come back to life. I felt the warm touch of the glass and I sighed with relief.

It must've only been a dream. A bad one.

I turned back to the window again, watching the early risers moving up and down the street. The snow wasn't falling this morning. The sun was finally coming out to greet everyone. I smiled.

"I'm going into town today, and I want you to come with me."

I looked at Blake baffled. He held out his hand for me to take.

I stood, still holding my drink close to me as if it was the only thing keeping me warm. I didn't care to touch his hand. Not ever. "I will be back to check on you within the hour. Don't make me wait, dear."

I gritted my teeth. "Where are you taking me?"

"I'm taking you with me to go shopping. I need to grab a few things in town and then we'll go into the Market. There's something there that I'm looking for, and it's very imperative that I get it today."

"Then why bring me along? Won't I just slow you down?" I took a long drink of the coffee, the liquid was turning lukewarm. Blake watched, his expression turning into something of awe.

He hadn't done any tests on me in a couple days. *What was he up to?*

"Quite the opposite. I have to confess that I do hate going out shopping by myself. I'd much rather have someone with me, preferably the company of a lady. Like yourself."

Gross. He looks twice my age.

"That's flattering and all but I'm not a doll. I'm half your age."

His wicked smile came out and he walked back to the doors. "On the contrary, my dear." He paused to open them looking back only a moment to say, "Now . . . don't forget. I don't like to be kept waiting."

Then he closed the doors and he was gone.

He seems way too chipper today, I think to myself. *Too happy.* It's not a good feeling that it leaves me with. Something bad is going to happen. Or has already happened. And I just have a feeling I'm not going to like it when he shows me.

  Like how we have different currencies for different places and countries, so does the country of Sintallious. It's understood that there are paper bills and written taxes known as "Charlatans"--the equivalent of waivers. Basically, those who have the money to buy waivers--or worm their way into the good intentions of the lords and king--can waiver anything they can get their hands on. Anything is up for grabs; including black market elixirs and potions as well as urbs and herbs that are illegal in certain parts across the country.

From "Mixed Studies"--SRP

Though the thought of going outside would be amazing, the idea of having to be around Blake the whole time didn't fit my stomach.

I should've asked him about Callie and Dean! I thought. He could have told me if they were coming. If Eric was coming.

"Ms. Cannon, are you even listening to me?!"

I pulled out of my thoughts. "Huh?"

Ms. Fitzgibbons was babbling on about the importance of respect when others are speaking to you. I couldn't disagree with her, but what she was complaining about was good enough to forget in thought. She was getting me dressed for the day's adventure with Blake as my guide.

Pulling one dress after the other, she finally chose one that suited her interest. A dark-gray wool dress that covered my arms and went all the way down to the floor. *I'm definitely going to be warm in this.*

"Which one looks better? This one, or this one?" She was trying to decide on which shade of gray cloak would work better with my already gray dress. *Yeah, my attention is not needed right now.*

She snapped her fingers in my face and I flinched back with annoyance. "What!?"

"Don't 'What' me, dear. This is important!" She had her hands on her hips, clearly caring way too much for something as small as outfit choices.

I rolled my eyes. "The shade shouldn't matter! My whole outfit is gray! I really don't care, just pick one!"

She huffed out angrily mumbling under her breath putting both cloaks back. She pulled out a different one. It was black. "Fine." she snapped "Black it is." Pulling it off its hanger she threw it around my shoulders. Then pulling the connecting straps that I didn't see, wrapping them in an 'x' position across my chest. It clicked together in the back securely.

"And take this as well." She handed me a fur wrap.

I held it awkwardly in front of me—not sure what I was going to do with it. "What should I do with it?"

Her eyes rolled. "Wear it obviously. It's a genuine fox fur scarf." She sounded pleased by the fact it was from a fox. "When the breeze bites at your neck, this," she pushed my awkward hands to my chest as if I were hugging it close, "will keep you warm. And if you put up your hood, then you won't have to deal with a Shiver Fever."

"Shiver Fever?"

She looked shocked that I didn't know. "A Shiver Fever is when you can't stop shaking, even when you're in a warm place. A fever takes hold and you become ill."

Like I couldn't have guessed that from the name . . .

I nodded my head and she motioned to the couch. "Now, let's tame that mane of yours."

Blake was knocking at the door right when Ms. Fitzgibbons was tying the end of my single braid with a bow. It was a frilly thing, plain white, but just the feeling of it in my hands reminded me of how much my own mother would braid my hair.

I miss those times. I want to go back.

Not anymore. They're gone, remember, Wanda?

Blake was looking me up and down with a sweet-sour smile. I had to swallow the acid in my mouth before it dumped all over the floor.

"It will do." He nodded his head and gestured for me to take his arm. "Come along. We mustn't dilly-dally."

He's definitely in a good mood today. Just a couple of days ago he was harsh and hard to read. His moves were unpredictable. But now, he's walking and talking like he had the best news given to him today.

What if it's about Callie and Dean? Are they both okay? I couldn't ask him now! He may turn sideways again. Punish me for speaking out of turn if he doesn't like what I have to say. I can't risk it. Not when I'm all by myself in this unfamiliar place.

I take my time moving around the couch, looping my arm around his. First I feel the heat. It makes me shiver as I grasp the fur scarf closer in my hands.

"Do you need my jacket, dear?"

He pulls me in closer to his side as we start our walk down the left hall, about to descend the spiral staircase. I shake my head. "No, no thank you. I'm fine. Really." I give him a tight smile.

He doesn't seem convinced, but let's it slide.

Then I smell his cologne.

We're descending the stairs. My nose pinches at the odor. This was the same odor I smelt at the dinner party with Callie and her uncle.

His cologne is toppling over me, overpowering my senses. I can literally feel my limbs numbing to the sense of his odor again. I remember asking Dean if he smelt it too? He nodded slightly.

It's richly sweet and unidentifiable. The only thing I can take from it is a twisted stomach that makes me sick and weak in the knees.

At the bottom of the stairs, we pass through a marble

foyer and walk out the two massive front double doors. The wind hits me next, harsh and unforgiving. Blake pulled me right up against him as we turned onto the left path, the double doors closing behind us.

"What a nice day indeed." He chimes. "Just perfect."

It's so cold! I haven't felt this way in so long! The feeling of the winter wind biting at my face and digging down my neck and down my back. It's so foreign and yet so familiar all at once. My spine tightens and I curl into his side. His odor is no longer there, but my limbs still feel numb. That, on top of the bitter touch of the winter air, really has me stumbling against Blake.

I was thankful he held me firmly to his side, or I would have definitely fallen a couple of times.

Thankful? What was I saying?

"Where are we going again?" I chided. Is this how he controls others like me, I pondered? Callie hadn't seemed bothered by it at all. *Were Dean and I the only ones smelling it?*

He gave a harsh sigh. "I need to grab some Charlatans in town. Then we're going into the market downtown to grab something of much value to me."

"What are you looking for?" I need to do anything to take my mind off the tight feelings that grow in my chest. It starts to become harder and harder to breathe in this weather.

"Something special." *He doesn't want to say.* I don't want to push any farther than need be. I need him to keep his temper in check today.

The realization of being outside finally hit me as we walked farther down the street. Looking around at the tall building made my jaw slack as I ogled at the sight. We were on *Urenbro Street* from what the sign at the corner said.

"Do you want one?"

I looked back to Blake. "Hm?"

He pointed to the small bakery shop at the same corner and saw the big sign in the window saying they were serving a new Carrot Cinnamon Bun. I didn't seem to care for food, but my stomach growled at the thought of eating one.

He checked both ways before pulling us onto the road and across the brick road. "C'mon, why don't we get some." I started to protest, but he added, "nothing beats a sugary sweet first thing in the morning."

I couldn't disagree. My stomach was lurching at me.

He tells me to wait outside the door for him. Not a few minutes later does he walk back out with two buns in one hand

and a small bag of pre-wrapped buns in the other. He passes one of the fresh buns into my hands as he frees his hand to wrap his arm around me again.

"If we stay on Urenbro, we'll be able to make it to the market in half the time. Though I can't say very nice things about the east side that much. It's one of the sketchier sides of the Market. So, stay close at all times." I looked up into his eyes. They're just as piercing and cold as the weather. I nod my head.

After we start walking, I take my first hesitant bite into the carrot bun. The sweet warmth of the cinnamon and the glaze on top made my stomach hum with satisfaction. There was only a small hint of a carrot taste but most of the time I couldn't even notice it.

"How is it?"

When I finished my last bite, I crinkled the wrapper into a ball and smiled. "Really good. Thank you."

He passed me the small bag of buns. "Here. You're welcome to have more."

I grabbed it hesitantly. "What's the trick?"

His light laugh made my chest ache. *Why is it so hard to hate him right now?*

"No trick. It's an even exchange." Both of us placed our wrappers inside the bag. "If there are no tricks from you, there won't be any from me. You have my word."

Why would I trust him? He's nothing more than a two-faced sociopath.

"Okay." I nod, grabbing the bag, digging inside for another bun.

After the last shop we exited I had finished my third bun. That was enough for me.

"Now we can head over to our last stop."

Blake took the bag full of buns from me and I wrapped my fur scarf around my neck. Tucking the ends under the belts, then pulled up my hood. Snow was starting to sprinkle down, the wind dying as more snowflakes fell. It was as if there was an invisible bubble around us, protecting us from the growing breeze outside us.

How is this happening? Am I doing this?

I glance sideways to Blake to see if he notices it as well, but he doesn't seem to see it. Or if he is, he isn't bothered by it. I feel glad at the thought.

He really is in a good mood today.

How long will this last, I think. It seems impossible for him to stay happy for too long.

I watched as he shoved the final cards in his coat pocket. He called them Charlatans, but I didn't know what that entailed. Were they coupons of some sort of an exchange or currency?

Mom carried a pouch of coins, but never cards.

Are they tickets for certain things?

I wanted to ask, but I held my tongue. Once we enter the east side of the Market, Blake is pulling me even closer to him as we move around traffic. My mind goes immediately elsewhere.

There are so many people here and the foot traffic is hard to maneuver around.

"Not a lot of people today."

I almost laughed at him. The street that the east market sits on is jam-packed with hundreds upon hundreds of people. The noise alone makes my ears warm from the cold. Merchants are yelling out deals to anyone passing by and everyone has their own conversations that carry onto others as we march forward.

Both of us are being shoved by busy people who don't care to apologize and we try to avoid most when we weave through different shops and alleyway merchants. Deals are being yelled at us left and right. People in fancy suits and dresses are laughing at things they whisper under their breaths. No one mines us or tries to pull us in as we pass—besides the cheat-selling merchants—and neither Blake nor I care to stand around and watch others.

He's on a mission and I'm just his company. I can see why that is. Even worse than that, I can feel it. Each minute that passes by that we are here, the more chance something dark and ominous will attack us. I don't know how to describe it other than the fact that everywhere we turn I feel as if I'm being watched. As if someone is lurking in the shadows just for us, waiting, plotting for our end when we decide to stop somewhere. It's like the feeling of never catching a deep enough breath.

Blake points to a small shop up the street. "There it is." We just turned the corner, and like the flip of the page, the crowds of people dissipated. Barely anyone walks the sidewalks and very few vehicles are parked on the side of the street like the street we were just on.

"Where are we?" I huff, trying to catch my breath.

We had slowed to a stop. The lights were out, and there was no sign to indicate someone was home. On top of the shop's sign was a single nest, its inhabitants gone for the season. All the letters that would be on the sign are nowhere in sight, the only thing left was the shadow of where they used to be. The name

"Pawn Shop" was forever etched into the stained wall.

Blake pushed in the door, an overhead bell ringing as the door closed behind us.

A faint, "I'm in the back!" echoed through the room.

Blake looked at me and gestured to the shop. "I have to take care of business. Look around or sit and wait for me. Don't go anywhere else." I bobbed my head as he rushed around shelves and displays, finally slinking into the shadows of a back hallway. There was the faint sound of a door opening and closing and I was finally alone.

The shop was small. Only four small aisles lined the floor, each shelf carrying something different. Toys, cups, jewelry, and more. It was like heaven really. I'd never stepped into a shop like this in my life. Not even earlier today with Blake. All of the shops from this morning were filled with furniture and light displays. Each of them organized to look like a waiting room.

There's a fireplace in the front left corner of the shop when you walk in and a thick rug. One chair sits in the corner but I don't take it. Right on the same wall stacks of books cover their shelves. Pulling the first one that catches my eye, I plop myself down in front of the lite fire and make myself comfortable. First I yank the scarf off and then the cape goes next, both of them in a pile in the single chair. Then once my boots are off I stretch my socked toes out to the fire to warm them back up.

On the front of the book's cover, it read, "The Adventures of James Rover." On the first page was a signature and a date. *July 3rd of 2064.*

Almost a hundred and forty years ago, I think to myself. The last date I saw was on a report from Brooks Tela-pad from Eric. It was the restriction report. I think the date was November 25, 2203? Or was it the 24th? I shook my head. *I can't remember.*

Flipping to the next page a small, tinted picture dropped into my lap. It was a black and white photo of a man in a camouflage outfit, and a young girl with a western hat and a solid color collar t-shirt and shorts. Both of them looked like adventurers excited for a new journey. Even though they looked beaten up and dirty, they still had large smiles on their faces.

On the back of the photo were two names. James Rover and Jane Rover.

Huh. They must be father and daughter. I smile at the thought before sticking the photo back and turning to the first page. It started with, "Once upon a time . . ."

Before I knew it, I was losing track of time. It was growing darker outside and the snow was falling heavier than before. Blake still hadn't come out of the back room and I was growing curious about what all he and the merchant were talking about back there. I almost stood to slink back there and peak, but I didn't want to move out of the comfort of the fire.

The journal I had been reading was still in my hand as I stood to watch the shadows outside. Only women in cloaks were passing by—their hoods far enough so that I couldn't see their faces—each and every one of them walking without company. And they remind me of ghosts with no direction.

Something drops from one of their cloaks. A small box.

I grab my things and stumble outside. "Hey!" I call out to her. "You dropped this!" She doesn't turn around. Neither does any of the other women.

A bell chimes a moment later and all of them turn in unison. They walk toward the chapel down the street.

Someone is ringing a bell--another woman in a cloak. Her face is covered too.

I fasten my scarf closer, shiver and look at the small box in my hand. On the tag, scribbled in thick ink, is my name.

"Wanda."

I whip around. Blake is scrambling down the steps, reaching for my shoulders.

"Are you okay?"

I furrow my brow, shoving the small box into my pocket.

I nod. Smile, "Of course," I push myself away from his hands. "Why wouldn't I be?"

His eyes are questioning. Looking back to the shop, then the chapel, and back to me. "Why'd you go outside?"

I notice the satchel hanging across his shoulders. I see the faint shape of a dark-stained wooden box inside and he shifts the bag behind him when he catches me looking. In a moment, my safety is no longer his first priority.

He continues. "What were you thinking? That you could simply walk around without a guide? You're a stupid, ignorant girl!"

I almost trip over my skirt as I take a step back.

His anger has finally flourished.

"I-I didn't mean to." I clear my throat. "I heard the bell ringing and I wanted to see where it was coming from."

He tilts his head.

Can he see through my fear?

"Did you see someone familiar? Someone, we both would know?"

"I'm not sure--,"

His hand is gripping the back of my neck. Cold and hard. "Don't play dumb,"

He snaps.

"I'm not!"

"Don't lie."

Anger was warming my face. For once I wasn't lying. And I was tired of stepping on eggshells.

"Let go of me!"

"Tell me," he grins. "Was it Alice? Gemma?"

I try to break the hold he has on me. It grows tighter.

I push my hands out to his chest fast. Scream, "Let, GO!"

The wind around us thrashes. His eyes were alight with a fiery blaze. "You wouldn't."

I *would* . . .

In a fierce, ruff exhale of air I shove my hands out letting my energy surge. The wind tightens around Blake in a tight whip of air and throws him across the street. His back cracks into the wall of an abandoned building and I gasped at the exhilaration.

All in one moment everything was calm.

Then--the air turned sour.

My chest tightened as he struggled to stand and walk forward. Panic filled my insides and I stumbled back to get as much space as I could between us. I had no energy to bring back more power, my body already depleted. "I told you to let go."

043

MESSAGE RECEIVED

Blake didn't talk to me the rest of the way back to the estate. And I didn't argue as he gripped my arm for dear life. He walked me to my room, closing the door with a slam.

Ms. Fitsgibbions didn't come in. Not a single peep from the halls outside my doors.

I stripped down and dropped my clothes on the floor in the bathroom. Pulling the nightgown over my head, I grab at the extra blanket on my bed and wrap it tightly around me. I was thankful Ms. Fitzgibbions had already started a fire before we got back, so once I got myself situated on the floor by the fireplace I pulled out the little box.

Ripping the tag off and throwing the lid into the flames, I dumped the contents of the box in my lap.

There was a note and a pendant necklace.

The pendant is small, flat, and round like a coin, which seemed to have metal fangs. At one end, the two points are sharp enough to cut into my palm as I gripped it tightly. Four small etched circles lined the middle of the metal in a row.

I opened the note, making sure to not grip the metal pendant too tightly.

Wanda--

We are so close I know it's undeniable you can feel our energy as we can feel yours. Though the distance and the time is long, we're almost there. We have included our signature pendant that allows us to find you a bit easier when your powers are severed long periods at a time. Use the pendant not only as a token of our close connection but for protection. Not only can you use it to take down a target but it can guide you to safety when you're lost. We will send more information when it's safe.

—A

Alice. I'm sure of it. When I read through it a second and third time I threw the piece of parchment into the flames. Once I watch the last of its ashes fall into the pit below the wood, I toss the pendant into the smoke. It topples to the bottom, ashes covering it in a sleek camouflage.

I can't risk having it on me. Not now.

I sigh, resting my head on my knees. The box, the tag with my name, and the note. They're gone.

The pendant still sits untouched under a pile of ashes. I close my eyes and grip the blanket tighter. *What happened today? That couldn't have been me . . . Could it? I wouldn't accept the idea.*

Knock, Knock!

I turn my back to the door, not bothering to answer. I'm too tired to argue. I just pull my knees in closer to my chest as I hide my face. When I hear my door opening and closing, heavy footsteps creep closer. I don't care to face him. Blake could do his worst.

"Wanda?"

My heart lurches.

"Are you okay?"

I turn and look fast. In all his glory, Eric stands over me, his eyes swimming in the familiar warmth I've grown to love. *Eric.*

I stand and slam myself into him before he can say anything else. My arms tighten around his waist and he lets out a deep laugh before wrapping his arms around me just as tight.

His embrace warms me through and through.

"You're here." I choke out.

"I could say the same." He chuckled. "Are you okay?"

I shake my head and dig my face into his chest trying to hide myself as much as possible.

"Do you want to tell me what happened while I was gone?"

"No." I pause. "I just want us to stay here forever. Let's do that, okay?" My body felt as if all my weight was pulled from my shoulders. My eyes felt heavy in a moment and I slipped to one side, my body finally catching up to my exhaustion.

"What you need is sleep," he says. I smile with agreement. I feel like I'm in the clouds. I'm calm. Free.

He shifted and scooped me up into his arms. My muscles didn't fight back and he walked me to my bed. Helping me under the covers, his arms lingered just enough for me to grip at his hand and hold him in place. "Don't leave me." I mutter. My eyes droop down and my head lulls to the side. "Not again."

My hand falls limp and I'm in and out of sleep. It's slowly dragging me under and I fight to stay awake a little longer.

Then, my bed dips and I can feel my body move as Eric

scoots in under the covers. I can hear his boots hit the floor and then I urge him closer to me. He doesn't hesitate wrapping me into his arms. My head sinks into his chest and I dip into the steady beat of his heartbeat. It thumps louder and louder as sleep consumes me. *I love you*, is what I think I hear him say.

I'm calm in a moment.

044

SINKING SMILES

[WANDA]

It's still dark outside as Eric is combing his fingers through my curls. And even though it's early in the morning, I feel as though I slept a thousand lifetimes.

"Tell me what's wrong." He whispers.

I dig my fear into his chest, his formal jacket gone. *He must have taken it off sometime in the night while I was asleep.* "Not until you tell me about Callie and Dean." I tighten my arms around his torso. The warmth of his body was numbing my limbs. "They had to have come with you."

His chest rose in a sharp inhale of air. "They did." His voice was solemn as he let out a deep sigh. "But it's not good."

I finally looked up at him. "What do you mean?"

His eyes were so dark—as if they were trying to hide something very dark inside. "When you were transferred out,

Blake did something."

Furrowing my eyebrows, I readjusted myself to sit beside him. I hugged a pillow close as I watched him. He didn't want to say anything. He looked afraid to tell me.

"Eric, what is it? Just tell me."

"Something happened to your friend Dean. He's okay. He's very healthy, but he's not the same person as he was before."

"What do you mean? Did something happen to his wound or something?"

The last time I saw him, he was still struggling with his gash. But that was a week ago. *Was it infected?*

He shrugged his shoulders. "I believe he could've been brainwashed. I don't really know. It's like he's lost all that made him himself. I pressed Blake for answers before he left and all that he said was that "it finally worked . . . and that now the real game could begin."

Brainwashed?! What did that mean? The game could begin? What game was he playing at?

I scramble out of bed. "Where's Callie? Has the same thing happened to her?"

What exactly was happening to my friends?

"Hold on." Eric stands, dashing out to block my path to the door. "What do you think you're doing? You can't go out there."

"Why not?" I grit my teeth. I shove at his chest to push him away but he doesn't budge. "I need to know she's okay! That she hasn't been—," my voice cracks, "That she hasn't been . . ." *hurt.*

Eric pulls me into his embrace. I try to pull myself away but he holds firm. "She's okay, Wanda. She's okay." He whispers it in my ear. "*She's okay.*"

"How do you know?" I sobbed. Tears weren't falling but my chest was breaking under the pressure. My mind was racing too fast for my body to catch up. "I need to see her for myself. Right now, I need to see her."

This couldn't be happening . . . First Dean. Now,--

Eric shook his head and sighed. He let me go. "She's been locked in her room all night. You can't see her until morning."

I huffed, turning away from him. Moving around the couch and dipping my hand into the ashes of the dead fire, I fisted the familiar metal pendant.

"What are you doing?" Eric's footsteps came closer and

I turned back to him, opening my hands. In my palms laid my pendant. "What is that?"

"Alice gave it to me."

His eyes widened. "You saw her?"

I shook my head. "No. But, Blake thought I saw someone. In the market we were at. Then I got irritated and--,"

His jaw popped side to side. "Blake told me. Before I came in to see you last night, he told us about what you did."

How I used my powers to throw him across the street and into a concrete wall.

For one split moment, I thought I had killed him. Calm waves rushed over me with relief, but then all the fear spiraled out when I watched him get up as if nothing happened. *I must've protected him when I threw him against the wall. That would explain why he didn't seem hurt in the slightest.*

Or he was using my powers against me. But that would mean he's an Anchor!

I squeezed the pendant tightly in my hands. "I was so conflicted by his emotions in that moment . . . I didn't like how he was speaking. I wanted him to stop so badly that I jus—I just pushed it all out."

He moved closer trying to pull me into another embrace, but I stepped away. Shook my head.

The pendant's teeth stabbed into my palm. I hissed, not realizing how tightly I'd been gripping it. Then it fell from my hand and clattered to the floor. He grabbed at my wet palm.

"Shit." He gasped.

My hand was starting to ooze out blood.

"I'll go grab the first aid kit. You sit down."

I didn't refuse. Sitting at the end of the couch, Eric dashed into the bathroom. He came back a minute later holding the small white box.

"You need to be more careful."

I shook my head as he cleaned the wound. "You shouldn't be here."

He pauses to look at me. "But I am. I don't want to be anywhere else."

I looked deep into his eyes. *I was searching for something. Peace of mind? Truth that this whole thing is just a dream.* He is all that I want to know, I think.

Is that what love is?

"We're so different from each other." I laugh.

He furrowed his brow. I sigh, squeezing my cut hand tightly around the cloth. It stung as I spoke. "We are so different from each other, and yet I feel we are more the same than I've ever felt with anyone else."

He doesn't move for a moment. It almost feels like forever.

Then he smiles warmly. "I feel the same for you."

I love you too, I want to say.

Knock, Knock!

"Ms. Cannon, are you up yet?" Ms. *Fitzgibbons*! I shove the first aid kit into Eric's chest. I stand, not knowing what to do. "Ms. Cannon," Ms. Fitsgibbons continues, "I'm coming in!"

I'm crossing my arms tightly when my doors open. I can hear Eric stand behind me.

"Good morning," I smile.

She's taken aback by Eric's presence as I thought, and looks between us suspiciously. "What's going on here?"

"I—uh," I showed my cut hand. "got my hand cut last night. I must've gotten it slashed when I threw Blake. Karma, I guess." I looked at Eric and cleared my throat. "Then he," I pointed to him, "came in this morning to check in on me."

It's as if Eric could read my mind. "I caught her trying to hide it from me as well."

She looked between us. Looking at Eric, she put her hands on her hips with a smirk. "Did she give you any problems?"

It was Eric's turn to look at me. He shook his head. "No." He looked back at her. "Not in the slightest."

The room filled with our silence as Ms. Fitzgibbons looked between us. When her eyes stopped on me, she spoke not to me, but Eric. "Let's speak in the hallway away from prying ears."

Eric gave a quick glance my way, shrugging his shoulders. I felt my face fill with concern. He held the door for Ms. Fitzgibbons and she closed it behind them. I took a cautious step forward. I didn't want to move any closer. Not if she could come in at any moment.

I look down and catch sight of my pendant. It's laying on the floor hidden slightly under the couch. I must've dropped it. And Eric probably pushed it under his boots when she came in. I silently say a thank you as I dip down to grab it back into my wounded hand.

I let it weigh there while I look at it. A hum numbs my palm. As if on cue, the air around the room twists around me. A storm was starting to brew and I closed my eyes to ignore it. My heart was racing again, my ribs aching with my heart pounding at them.

What are they talking about out there? They're talking about me, yes, but about what? Would Ms. Fitzgibbons tell Blake about this? What would he do if he found out? Would he hurt Eric?

I took a deep breath trying to calm the wind, but it only escalated. No matter how much I tried to calm my head *and* my heart at the same time, there was no stopping the energy around me. No escaping my invisible cage.

"Wanda!"

I opened my eyes and looked at the figure. Eric.

"Take a deep breath!" He shouted over the wind. I hissed as I crushed the pendant in my hand. I felt the blood pool out again. I could only watch as Eric rushed around the floating furniture, grabbing at my arms. His touch was a fuel in itself, my powers growing.

"You need to go."

He pulled me down hard. He locked my body against his as the storm began to calm down. Now I get it. Once the air stopped completely my chest cracked with hurt. I exhaled.

"Breathe, Wanda. Just breathe." He was whispering it in my ear. "Breathe."

Dean said he was my Anchor.

I shouldn't be worried about Blake finding out about last night. *I should be worried about what he has Eric doing to me . . . to my powers.*

SOMETHING'S WRONG

[WANDA]

Eric left after Blake came in. And after I calmed down, that didn't take too long. Ms. Fitzgibbons had rushed to get Blake when she saw. Eric was asked to explain.

"She started to float off the floor and a tornado whipped through the room moving all the furniture around."

Plain and simple. Sadly that meant when Blake came rushing in a panic, he had that damn velcro band in his hand. He didn't even hesitate to put it around my left arm.

I hissed at him. "You can't wait until I'm dressed before you put this on?"

"No." he sat himself in one of the chairs that had moved to the foot of my bed.

"Your not gonna leave?" I growled.

He waved my anger away like it was nothing. "Just relax. I'm not even here."

"But you are." I huffed.

Dropping the hope that he'd leave, I sink into my usual window seat. This time I'm on the other side, my back facing him and the door.

I couldn't stop my mind from wandering to my pendant. Eric took it out of my hand before Blake could see it and shoved it into his pocket. I didn't refuse because I couldn't get caught with it or I'd be in trouble. But the fact I didn't have it in my hand still made my nerves spike. That or the lack of blood was messing with my head.

Knock, Knock!

I didn't have to turn my head to know it was Ms. Fitzgibbons. She was setting a tray on my table that was now by the fireplace.

I heard another pair of footsteps and I turned to see someone else coming in.

"Sir, she's been refusing to eat all morning." Dean.

I stood fast and stared at him. He didn't seem fazed by me looking and turned his attention to Blake who was sitting at the table. He had his own plate that he was digging into.

"And?"

"Sir, she's refusing to eat."

Blake and I locked eyes. His smile was in between maniacal and wicked. I walked up slowly to Dean and he shifted uneasily to the side. He gave me a disgusted look and I had to swallow my throat to avoid screaming. I looked at Blake again and gritted my teeth.

"You're a real piece of work, aren't you? Brainwashing my friends now?"

He doesn't seem fazed. "Please, dear. Come sit down before your food turns cold."

I stick my nose up at the bowl of eggs and sausage. "I'm not hungry." But I wanted to really say, *If I get any closer to you, I'll be throwing up some real nasty words.*

His jaw tightened into a serious tone. "Either you eat or you don't for the rest of the day. It's your choice."

I fist my hands and take a step forward. "No. If she doesn't eat, I won't either."

"I told you what I would do if you didn't listen to me."

"And I'm telling you, no."

My head was pounding with the lack of blood flow. I could feel my face draining of color slowly.

I'm about to faint, I think.

Just because Blake's band could take the place of an Anchor doesn't mean I couldn't still muster the strength to stand up to him.

His jaw tightened when he swallowed. "Dean, make sure Ms. Underwood is locked in her room for the time being. I'll be down later to switch with you." Our eyes never break eye contact. *He's daring me to make a move.*

To lash out.

I hold my ground as Dean shifts. "What about her?" He nods to me.

I tighten my jaw. Tilt my head.

Blake says: "You'll watch her tonight. It'll give Kane and Florbal a couple hours to rest for once."

"Understood, sir."

I narrow my eyes. *What have you done to him,* I think.

Don't be frightened.

My heart trips forward. I step back.

Another person enters the doorway.

"Sir!" *another soldier.* "He's arrived."

Trust in me.

I shake my head. Regret it as I stumble forward. My head's pounding too loud. My vision is starting to blur. I close my eyes to steady myself.

Wanda! Screams the vague echo of a familiar voice.

Is *that Callie's voice?*

Air whips past me. I hear a loud thud rupture my skull.

Nothingness follows.

046

MORE THAN ME

[ERIC]

I'm only allowed to stand outside her door. And Harrington is inside, making sure she doesn't get into trouble.

"Having fun yet?"

I fold my arms. "Shouldn't you be watching Underwood?"

Kane shakes his head. Reaches for the door handle.

I block him fast. "What're you doing? You can't go in there."

"Let him pass."

My heart stops at the thunderous voice. King Peter stands behind Kane, walking up to us slowly.

His black suit makes him seem menacing. "Sir--,"

I step back, my skin draining. Kane smiles. Opens the door.

I keep my eyes glued to the ground.

"I understand why you worry about her."

I look up, "What do you mean?" Kane is walking back into the hall, Wanda in his arms. I take a cautious step forward, and stop when I notice the King staring. "What are you going to do?"

"Does it really matter?" Kane chimes. Harrington follows behind quietly, his frame more tense than before. Once both of them are turning the corner, I look back to the king.

"You can't hurt her."

He smiles. "I have no intention to."

My jaw tightens. *Did you have any intention to hurt my sister?*

"I sense you don't like me. And I understand."

I shake my head. "No you don't."

"If you don't trust me, you can be with her."

"Is that some kind of threat?"

His laugh is deep and throaty. Equally light. "No. I just understand that a man like yourself would rather be in the room if something happens. Blake told me you feel something deep for this young girl. And not because you're an Anchor."

I tilt my head. "What's going to happen to her?"

"Nothing that you won't know of."

047

COMPLICATIONS

[LEAH]

When Blake had his men raid the chapel, that was our cue to flee into the shadows. Like always.

And of course, with little success in capturing "Alice and her Renegades" news spread across the market like a wildfire. Not only were the rebels in town. So was the King.

But Alice knew of this. I don't know how she does it, but after reawakening her powers, all of her senses of every magical being have heightened. Including the power to sense when the king was close. He's powerful. One of the strongest people with magic. Yet he never uses it.

"If you had let me grab her while I was right in front of her, we wouldn't have to be dealing with *this*."

This, meaning the King.

Gemma couldn't seem to get a grip on the fact that Alice

had a plan. That--

"We can't get caught, Gemma. You know that." Alice snaps. "Blake was right there! He would've called for backup."

"I could've knocked him out, easy."

I let out a sarcastic laugh. "Then we'd have a battle on our hands. You know we're not well liked here. People would've gotten hurt."

She doesn't seem to care. Rolls her eyes and folds her arms in a pout. "You'll never trust any of my plans."

"Because you don't care about anyone other than yourself."

Her jaw tightened. "I guess it's a good thing I didn't tell you then."

I narrow my eyes. "Tell us what?"

"What did you do?" Alice snaps.

She shrugged. "You sent Misty out to watch from a distance. Not to mention you told her she was the best one out of all of us to not be detected by the King."

That was true. Misty was the weakest--if I had to say it

so bluntly--out of all of us, making her the best one to fly under the radar. Not only that, but she had the ability to manipulate space around her.

Simply put: she could be invisible if she wanted to.

With of course the added bonus that she could mold the wind to her will like Wanda.

Gemma could do it too, but not as powerfully as Misty or Wanda.

"You told her to go *inside*?! Are you trying to get her killed?"

I step forward to grab Alice. To calm her.

She heaves a large breath before stepping back again. "Get her out."

Gemma shook her head. "She told me if she did this, she wouldn't leave until everyone was out safely.

Damn you!

"Gemma, get her the hell out now!" Alice snapped.

"I can't go in without getting myself caught. You said it yourself. No one gets captured again."

Not again, her voice rings through our heads.

Not again, Gemma and I repeat back.

048

DISTURBANCE

[WANDA]

Blake's hand never leaves my arm. "They should be here. Where are they?"

I shrug my shoulders. "I don't know." I lie.

Blake and I were deep into the jungle now. If I knew any better I would use my powers to shove him to the side and run as far as I could away from him. But, there was no use. We were in the dream world. No matter how far I made it away from him, he'd still be right beside me in the real world.

He shook me. "Where are they?!"

"I don't know! Really!"

He pulled us into the closest clearing. "Call them out. Now! Call them out!"

I flinched away from his impatience and huffed a shaky

breath.

Where are they?

It's getting harder to stay focused here. I'm too tired. Tired . . .

"Call them forward!" He yelled.

"GEMMA!" I screamed. "ALICE!" Only the echoes followed. "IS ANYONE THERE!?"

Nothing.

"Damn it." He hissed. "Where could they be?"

Find them.

Something sharp pierced my arm and my knees gave into the pain. I knew the band was around my arm, but when I looked at it, it wasn't there. It doesn't show up in the dream world, I remind myself.

"Get up."

I shook my head as I let my body melt into the dirt. It was oddly warm and comforting. Too tired, I thought.

This isn't working, Blake. Come back.

I didn't even care that the voice wasn't my own. I agreed with the thunderous dismay.

Yes, *please*.

Another pinch at my arm and my eyes were opening out of the dreamscape. In a moment my body shoots up, my lungs gasping for air.

I wanted to scream.

"Take a deep breath. It's going to be okay. Just breathe."

Eric.

He rushed to my side from somewhere—*How long had he been here for this?*—and I curl my body up to his. He wraps his arms around me and I close my eyes to shut the rest of the world out.

Strange you are . . .

"That is some impressive work you've got there, Blake."

"Thank you, sir. I couldn't have done it without your help."

The man's deep laugh could shake the room's foundation. "No, no. It was all you. Brilliant work! Truly!"

"Thank you, sir." There was a pause and I knew he was looking at me. Both of them were. "Though, next time I should give a smaller dosage. She doesn't seem to be taking it well."

Eric's throat clears. "Might I suggest that she takes time to rest? Her body can only take so much."

"Of course," King Peter chimes. "I advise you to take care of her for the time being."

I could feel Eric's arms tighten around me slightly. "Yes, sir."

"Don't let anyone disturb her. Is that understood?"

Rest now, child.

"Clear as air."

I couldn't stop shaking. I was pooling with sweat. Digging my head deeper into Eric's chest I heave heavy breaths. It's taking the rest of my strength to push King Peter's thoughts out of my head. The weight of them is too much for me to handle. I can't stay awake any longer.

I feel Eric's arms shift under my back and under my knees as he lifts me off the table. I hear the creak of a door and then the icy touch of a hand on my cheek. Blake.

I turn away. My eyes sinking.

Quiet thoughts clear my head.

Rest now.

..

049.

TWO HEADED SNAKE

[WANDA]

The first sensation I was getting was being cold. Very cold. Snow was falling all around me. I could feel each and every flake melting into my skin.

Where was I?

You are in my home.

I open my eyes. Around me stands the ruins of an old castle.

But it's in shambles, I think out to the voice.

"It is beautiful, is it not?"

Flashes pass through the back of my head. The voice, familiar. Known.

"You," I look around in the fog. "King Peter. You're the one

I hear in my thoughts."

"Smart girl."

You know something I don't.

I shake my head. "I don't know what you're talking about? You're in my head." *This is just a dream meant to look like the dreamscape.*

"But this is the dreamscape."

No. "It doesn't snow there. I'm dreaming."

His monstrous frame formed into the mist a few feet away from me. I jumped back in surprise. *How'd he do that?*

"The dreamscape isn't one place, Ms. Cannon," he continues. He's holding his hand out for me to grab. "It can be any place where a power core is strongest. And right now, I'm the strongest thing here."

I shake my head, standing on my own. "They never told me you had powers of your own."

"Who?" he questions. "Ms. Walker? Blake?"

I nod.

"I don't mean to hide it from anyone."

I could feel my heart slowing. It was getting harder to breathe in the high altitude.

I look around. "If this isn't your palace . . . What is this place?"

Home.

"You said that already. It doesn't make any sense."

Neither do you.

I close my eyes. Try to clear my head to no avail. "If you have your own magic, why do you need ours? You can get to the temple without help. Why kill people for theirs?"

His face turns icy. "I don't kill people."

"Say that to Eric."

In my daze of sleep, he had revealed that when he got home, his sister had already been taken. He said the Meds wouldn't let him see her. They wouldn't show him where they buried the bodies.

I had cried quietly into the blanket between us, not wanting him to know I heard the whole thing.

"Your Anchor."

I nod. "His sister was finally getting better. And who knew if she'd make it through if you hadn't stolen her like so many others. Stealing from them, and burying them in shallow graves somewhere. That's what you do, *great king*." I mock. "You take, and take, and take--just to get your fill. Then you laugh and spit in their graves when they fail you."

He's shaking his head, a storm slowly brewing around him. "That's not true. None of it."

"Then check the reports for once. Blake must be the true king here. Not you." My expression turns sour. "You're no king of the people. You're a coward."

"No."

I fist my hands, shaking with the restricted powers begging to be let out. "Let those people go. Let Alice and the others go. Let my friends go." he's backing up, shaking his head vigorously. "Let me go."

His frame stiffened. Ridged as a boulder, I can see the fire burning in his eyes.

You're wrong. Ms. Walker didn't see it. Ms. Underwood didn't see it. You don't see it--

Look!

His voice ruptures the very ground below us. I stumble and crash to the clear glass that clears itself for me.

I gasp. "What the--!"

It's a graveyard. A pit of bodies unnamed.

This was below us the whole time!?

I almost want to hurl. "You did this. All these people . . . *oh my*--you killed all these people!"

He's starting to laugh. Shaking his head with a hysteric chuckle.

The bones are starting to shake with the rest of the ruins. *What is he doing?*

I can't breathe.

Am I next!?

His eyes turn to me. They're black.

He steps forward and I wave my arms in a back sweep for my powers to push him back.

Just like I did Blake.

It had no effect.

I did it again. And again.

Nothing.

"You can hit me with all the power you have and you'd still be unable to move me." he chided.

I gritted my teeth. "Watch me."

I knew deep down he was trying to keep me here as long as he could. I didn't understand why. And I didn't want to find out. I wasn't going to let him hold me down anymore.

I took a deep breath, closing my eyes. The roar of the wind around us was deafening. Ear-piercing as if the bones of the dead still had voices to call out to me. I can feel the hairs on my body standing up, forced by the tension between the King and I.

I'd never woken up before, but if I tried, I could do it. I just needed to focus.

Focus on what?

Get out of my head!

Focus,

Focus!

FOCUS!

I gasp.

Eric!

050

ECHOES

ERIC!

It's as if bees are buzzing in my head. Not to mention the snake burrowing himself in my skull. I can hardly concentrate.

"Get out . . . of my head." I groan.

"Not until you tell us where you got these papers." Blake shakes them in my face.

My head is pounding. I can't move without making myself nauseous. "I won't."

Blake's hand strikes my face abruptly. My vision blurs and my throat contracts. "Tell me!" he barrels out.

Tell him.

Tell him.

Submit!

Tell him!

Dean's voice is slowly cracking through my defenses.

ERIC!

No. I can't do this!

"Please," I hiccup. "Stop this." Straining myself against Dean's hands at my back, I try to calm myself. Voices are swarming every piece of me. "I can't think straight."

Blake's jaw rotates slowly, as if pondering the release.

"No. Not until you tell us who gave you the papers."

I shake my head. "You already know!"

"Then remind me! Did a ghost give you these?" he mocks.

Spit is coating my throat as the tears are pooling down.

ERIC!

My eyes widen at the familiar voice. I know that voice! And I'm sure Dean can hear it echo through my mind as I focus on it.

Say it again, I think back. Say it again!

ERIC!

Blake is looking between the two of us. "What's happening? What is she saying?"

Dean releases me and stands. "It's Ms. Cannon, sir."

Blake looks down at me. I heave a shaky breath as the buzzing has stopped. "Something's wrong."

"Why is there blood on it?"

"Wanda cut herself on it." Eric whispers.

"And why are you giving it to me again?" I question. "Aren't you on Blake's side? Is this some kinda trick?"

"No trick." he forces the pendant into my hands. "Just keep it safe for her. If Blake was to find this on her, I don't know what he might do next . . ."

My head was in a daze as Wanda's voice kept on repeat in my head. Something wasn't right for sure. Blake had been the first one to enter her room, and Dean and I were last. And it took the rest of my energy not to dive for her.

Wanda was standing across from Eric--like a standoff.

Everything in the room was shaking. But that wasn't the thing that was wrong.

"What the hell--!" Blake commanded. "What happened? Why are her eyes glowing--?"

Her eyes. That's what was wrong.

Pure white and glowing. And not only that--

Her gaze shifted toward Blake's voice. She stepped forward but Eric blocked her path and she stopped again. Looked at him questioning.

Don't do this, Eric.

He's blocking her path! Why?

"What's happening, Florbal. Answer me!" Blake snaps.

The air swelters around us. Eric says, "Something happened between the king and Wanda. She hasn't calmed down since she woke up."

"She was able to speak with him? How?" Blake questions.

"She said the dreamscape!" Eric gasps. His face contorts and I move to see his expression. His eyes are going in and out of the same glow as Wanda's.

Is she trying to control him?

"She wants to enact revenge."

"Then stop her!"

I can help, I think out. Let me help!

Dean grips my arm harder with no response.

"I can't!" Eric groans.

"Then I will!" Blake strides forward.

"No!" He blocks him.

"I can't let anything happen to her." That's what he said to me. *"She's all that matters in this world to me now."*

I close my eyes. Focus my mind toward Wanda.

Can you hear me? I ask.

"Don't interfere." Wanda speaks to the room.

Please! Tell me what happened. I might be able to help.

Her head shakes. "Don't interfere."

"Who is she speaking to?" Blake questions.

"Underwood," Dean answers. "She's trying to communicate with her."

If only I knew my powers. I could try to stop this. Calm Wanda if I could. "Let me help, Wanda. Stop this."

They all deserve to die for the lives they've taken! Every last one of them!

"You saw the graveyard." I shrink back against Dean. His arm wraps around my middle as I can feel my body give to the weight of the memory. "I saw it too." King Peter tried to communicate with me through my thoughts. But all I heard were the faint screams of people burning. I remember the slight breeze when the fire roared. Whispers were weaving around me. Names. Some unknown. Some familiar.

Blake is looking for your friends. They're in trouble.

Her laugh echoes through the room. "They don't stand a chance against us."

We can't do this on our own, I think. The risk is too high.

"They're here."

Wanda's eyes flicker. Eric takes the moment to grab her around the middle. "What'd you say?" she whispers. Her eyes are falling back to normal.

I loosen my hold on the pendant in my hand. Let it slip into view of everyone in the room. Its row of symbols on the metal glowing a sharp orange.

She gasps.

"Where'd you get that?" Blake steps forward. I pull it out of his grasp.

"Alice gave it to me." I lied. "Told me it was her way of letting me know she was here."

Eric's eyes narrowed in confusion.

"I believe the second time Wanda cut her hand, the pendant glowed. I came back to check on her, only to find that it was all healed up." he said.

"What does that mean?"

He shrugged his shoulders. "It could mean a number of

things. But the only thing I can think of is that it's a power source. Something to absorb magic and give it when needed."

"You think it healed her?"

Blake forces my hand open to take it. He looks at it keenly.

Then he's looking between everyone. "Florbal, you're with me. Kane's on his way."

"I won't--,"

"It's an order, soldier."

Eric...

Wanda's voice still beams around the room. She doesn't want him to leave her.

Dean still hasn't released me. I stiffen as he pulls us back from the doors. Wanda doesn't move as Eric leaves. Her eyes aren't on him anymore.

There on me.

051

DOUBLE OR NOTHING

[MISTY]

I grip the pendant tighter. The glow is warming my arm as I slip around the corner.

No one can see me.

"You can't do that!"

"This isn't the first time this has happened. And I'm not letting it happen again."

Blake's voice is a chill down my spine as I look toward his direction. He's speeding down the hall, something tightly wound in his hand.

"What'd you mean, *this has happened before*? She's not some animal to be put down. She's a person."

Eric Florbal. *Why is he trying to argue with him?*

Where's Wanda?

They both enter a room. There is shuffling before I hear Wanda's friend scream. "WANDA!"

I dash forward and stumble as to not run into the soldiers in uniform. The room is flung around.

Eric's hand is gripping Blakes arm. "What have you done!?"

Blake is threatening him to get off. He doesn't budge. A soldier strides forward then, fighting to get Eric out of the room.

The Transparent is holding the girl back as she cries out. "YOU MONSTER! WHAT HAVE YOU DONE!?!"

He's different, I think.

"Don't make me do it to you as well!" Blake snaps back. "Know your place!"

The girl is starting to choke on her sobs as the only thing she can do is slump to the floor and cry. The Transparent doesn't let her go.

What has happened?

I turn to the bed. Blake is pulling Wanda up into his arms. A black band is wrapped around her arm with something sticking slightly out of it. I can't identify it, but note it as both of them leave the room.

Gemma said Wanda was the main priority. But my mind was made up at the moment.

I turned back to the girl--Wanda's friend, Callie.

The transparent--Dean I believe?--releases her after a moment, and steps toward the door.

Wanda . . . I hear Callie whisper through her thoughts.

Wanda, I repeat back. She's in trouble.

Her eyes dart around the room. Looks outside as she shakes her head.

Where are you?

I take another look at the transparent. His eyes are looking around the room as well.

Can he hear me? I question.

"Sadly, I'm the only one you can hear, Dean."

I nod. Understood.

My heart is racing . . .

Stop him.

She smiles at the ground. "And I'm going insane. I can't get out of here without her. We stick together."

"In your dreams, Underwood." Dean huffs. "Don't make this any harder on yourself. Cannon made her choice."

I loosen the pendant in my hand. Callie stands.

This is gonna burn. Hold out your hand.

She loosens her hands at her sides and I clasp it with the pendant between us. Her jaw tightens at the unfamiliar warmth.

"What the hell--!"

Both our eyes turn to Dean. He's looking at us. Both of us.

"You can see me--," I start.

"Don't move!"

I tilt my head.

Are you quick on your feet? I ask Callie.

Yes.

"Good." I release our hands and allow the air around the room to build slowly. I've come so far that it comes naturally to me when I think about it. I fist my hands and ready my air control on one central point--Dean's chest. "Keep up."

He's rushing forward--as if in slowmotion--and I exhale the power, allowing myself to knock him clean off his feet. His air becomes mine as he collides with the wall.

"How the hell did you do that? You were so fast!"

Practice.

I shake my head, striding to the door. I waved her forward. "Come on. I told you to keep up."

"What about him?"

I look back at her friend. Smile at my quick work of him. "We'll pick him up on our way out. He'll be fine for now."

She nods. "Alright. I'm following you then."

You've gotta tell me how you did that?

Did what? I question.

How you got in here. One minute, you were in my head and in the next, you were right in front of me.

We pause as her guide turns the corner. He doesn't see us, and we slip past.

How'd you do that? She repeats.

"Quiet."

She pauses behind me. "Why are we here?" she whispers.

I roll my eyes.

I spent two days here. Scoting and observing every move of the coming-and-going soldiers. I knew whatever I did first, my second step needed to be the same.

Getting Eric Florbal on my side.

And from seeing how he treats Wanda . . . it won't be too hard to convince him.

He loves her . . .

Callie's air hitched for a moment. She doesn't want to trust anyone who wears uniform colors.

No one can blame her.

I take my pendant back and focus my hands around its mold.

"What are you doing?"

"Shut up." *I'm trying to focus . . .*

The edges sharpen and I sigh as I reveal the new object in my hand. A slim blade.

I can hear Callie's questions bubbling up again. I try to ignore them as I jam the tip into the lock. The compression of air between the two fills my ears as it snaps open.

Callie opens the door for me, and Eric is ready. He springs forward only to stop mid-swing.

"Underwood!" he exhales. "I thought you were--!" his eyes met mine. "You're--,"

"Yeah. And you're gonna help us get Wanda out." I make space for him to follow. "Now let's go."

"Where are the others?"

He's asking about Alice, Leah, and Gemma. I grip the pendant close, cutting the permanent scar on my hand. I hear both of them hiss as I do it. "They'll be here."

How do you know that?

I pause at the end of the hall. Check for clearance. No

one's around.

I stab the pulsing blade into the floor. My blood is soaking into the wood. "This will tell them."

"Is it some kind of portal or something?"

I give Eric a questioning look. "That's not possible."

Callie snickers. "And magic is? Yeah, okay. Sure."

"Do you guys have a plan?"

I shake my head. "If I knew I would tell you. But I don't."

As I pull a packed strip of cloth out of my side pocket, Callie proceeds to stress the air in her chest. "What do you mean? You don't have a plan!? Then what was that blueprint for? It had Alice's insignia on it. Are you saying you just drew up a map for fun?"

Seeing how I planted the fake plans in her room to cause a stir--I don't care to carry my breath out. "Yep."

"And we're supposed to just wait here until the others come?"

"Nope."

"You can't seriously be saying, we have to wing it."

I shake my head. Sigh.

"Say something." Callie grabs my shoulder. *Say something.*

"I thought you were quick on your feet? Not nitty-nanny."

Her jaw tightened.

"He's gonna take her back to Hightown if we don't stop him."

I look at Eric. The air around him is filled with sorrow. Something bad has happened, I observe. Someone close has passed. Family, I think.

"Why?" I question, "I overheard you. He said it happened before. What did?"

Wanda . . . Callie sighs.

"Wanda was out of control." Eric starts.

She had glowing eyes . . .

"Glowing eyes?" I look between them both. Alice had an episode like that. But it only came about when she first interacted with the king in the dreamscape. She woke up in a rage. It was as if a fiery blaze was flaring out of her eyes. "What color was it?"

"White." they both answered.

Alice's were green. Strange. I'll make note of that for later.

"Alice had the same thing happen to her."

"What did Blake do?"

I shake my head.

"It wasn't him that did anything. It was her. She caused an explosion. All of us took that chance to run."

"That's how you escaped?"

I nod.

Silence fills the space around us, and I look around again. There are very few soldiers here. Either that means, they're short staffed--which I highly doubt--or they are all collecting themselves somewhere else.

No matter how much I want to wait for Alice and the others to get here, I can't just stand here. I need to think . . . *think . . . move!*

"We need her to blow up some stuff."

"We're actually gonna do something?"

"How do we do that?" Eric interrupts.

"Simple." I grip my wrapped hand several times. "We make her mad."

"And how the hell are we gonna do that? We don't even know where she is."

"She's in a lab down stairs." Eric speaks.

I nod. "Perfect. Lead the way."

You still haven't answered my question. Callie huffs as we run forward--Eric taking the lead.

We don't have to do anything. Blake will do it all himself.

We share a smile.

This is gonna be fun!

Indeed, I think. And while we're doing this, it'll give the others time to catch up.

052

FOLLOW

[ALICE]

"He's gonna weigh us down."

I roll my eyes. "Either you help me, or you can sit your ass outside and be our look out."

Gemma's fists clench and unclench for a moment. "Fine."

One of the boy's arms is around my shoulder. The other is around Gemma's. I nod to her as we make our way down the hall. Leah's made it clear that she's better outside. So I let my worries slide as I know she'll be here when we make it all out.

Don't get caught. Her words echo out.

I snicker. *Never.*

Our pendants glow when we near Misty's. "Where do you think she would've gone?"

I shake my head. "I don't know."

Is she here?

I nod. "I can feel her nearby. Callie and Wanda too. But something is interfering."

"What do you think it is?"

Blake, I think out.

"No doubt there." She adjusted Dean's weight onto her back. "How do you wanna go about this then?"

My nerves spike as memories surface. I swallow them, trying to focus on anything but . . .

"Don't move!"

Our heads twist to the soldier. His holster is empty, the slim pistol in hand.

Let me take him out.

I shake my head. Raise my hands in surrender.

We need to find Misty and the others first.

"Drop the dagger!" the soldier snaps.

Gemma lets Misty's pendant clatter to the floor.

Let him find them for us . . .

053

DELUSIONS

[WANDA]

"Truth or dare?"

I remember this memory . . . I said: "Truth!"

Callie's face flushed before looking away. "Don't lie, okay?" I remember she was really nervous. "Do you like Dean?"

Of course.

Even to this day, *"Are you crazy? He's like a brother! Yuck!"*

She punched my arm.

That really did hurt. *"What was that for?"*

I knew she loved him. It was the way she looked at him. Into his calming pools, everything around her melting away as if nothing else mattered.

Eric?

Anyone?

Am I really alone? Again?

My memory mists away to reveal another. It's like my mind wants me to watch every part of my life, from every moment that I missed out on.

But I *was in all these?*

How long had I been asleep for? I don't even remember dozing off.

Wanda.

Is someone there?

Wanda! Wake up!

Who's this? Is this my consciousness waking me up?

WAKE UP!

054

BREAK TWO

[CALLIE]

All we gotta do now is get the hell out.

"I'll get him," Eric nods to Dean. "You take Wanda."

I tighten my jaw.

"Let's get them out," he reassures. "Okay?"

I nod, pulling Wanda's arms around my neck. Even though she can't move, I know she's conscious again.

Whatever Blake gave her, also stunned her body so it wouldn't be able to move even if she woke up for any reason.

Eric is flinging Dean around his shoulders as Alice commands the room. "Let's go! We don't have much time!"

Misty and Gemma are making quick work of the oncoming soldiers, and we all hustle to keep up with our group.

I can't move . . .

I adjust Wanda at my back. "I know," I huff. "Only a little bit longer, okay?" We take a sharp corner back to the front of the estate. "We're almost home-free."

She can't seriously be taking us through the front, can she? I think to myself.

Misty is the one to swing the doors open.

Apparently so.

"Where's Leah?" Gemma calls.

Alice huffs, "She should be here."

I turn back to check on Dean.

"Wait!" I cry. Neither of them are in sight. "Where'd they go? They were right behind me!"

Eric? Wanda is stirring.

I nod to confirm her confusion, and then the air sharpens. I can feel her body around me warm.

Eric, she repeats again. I know the other girls hear her too, as they look at her the wind whips around us.

Surrender.

My head turns the way we came.

Surrender. Now.

Dean's voice through my head is like the start of a headache. I push it away, fighting to listen.

"We need to go," Misty pulls. "Now."

Not without him. Wanda snaps.

Drop her.

I shake my head. No!

Eric steps through the shadows first. Then the barrel of Dean's gun on him is in view. Then he's there, Blake by his side.

"You don't want to do this," Blake smiles.

I shake my head again. "Let him go."

"You don't want this man. He's betrayed his team. He's--,"

"Not Eric." I heave. "Dean."

No . . . Wanda moans.

I *must do this.*

I hear Alice step closer to us. "Let him go, Blake. Both of them. This isn't right."

"And you are?" He counters.

Leave.

Alice's voice through my head is much sweeter than anyone else's. But the sting at the end of each word is like poison. "I'm not leaving without him," I hiss.

Have it your way.

"Alice!" our heads turn to the voice. It's the other girl-- Leah. "We've gotta go--!" Her face grows pale at the sight before her.

Alice takes a step closer toward Blake. Dean shifts the pistol into Eric's side more. "No sudden moves, or I shoot."

Her hands are up in surrender.

"Just let them go, Blake."

"Give up, Walker. You have no authority here."

"Let them go, and I'll stay. Does that sound like a fair wager?"

I can hear the girls behind me shift forward in unison. Blake sees this too. We all know he's got the floor for a response.

"Depends if you think you're worth two lives," he snickers.

I take slow steps backward so as to not shift focus away from her. I can't leave Dean here, but I also can't let Wanda be caught. Not when we're so close. When she's so close to being free.

"I'd bet my life is nothing more than the other people you experiment on, but it's all fun and games to you. So, it really doesn't matter, does it?"

Dean's hand grips the gun tighter. **Don't move.**

I freeze.

"Get out of here." Eric hisses. "All of you."

Eric . . .

"Keep her safe."

Run, Alice is chiming over and over again. **Get ready to run. Run!**

Eric's body shifts then, and Alice takes the movement to rush forward.

Two consecutive shots are fired.

DON'T MISTAKE THIS AS THE END

[CALLIE]

Several Hours Later . . .

The campfire is the only thing keeping us apart, the heat a burning reminder that this is my fault. And I don't blame her for not wanting to talk to me. But her silence just makes my seldom thoughts more horrific at the situation.

We made it out of town.

"It'll only be two days more," Alice says. "Take the time to rest now before morning."

"I can't wait to sleep in my own bed." Gemma comments. "This whole trip has taken a lot out of me."

You're not the only one, I think.

Forcing myself to close my eyes, the scene reemerges. Alice running forward for the gun. The gun firing. The blood pooling at each of their sides—both Alice's and Eric's. He got most of the blow, falling to the ground in a heap.

Wanda had screamed. Full-voice, all body motion pulling herself away from me like flight. Her eyes went fiery orange, glowing more intensely than before. Then the room became a hurricane as Alice struggled back and away, trying to get Wanda down at the same time. I was no help when I took my chance to reach for Dean in the chaos. He shoved me back, his eyes flickering in and out with Wanda's glow.

I could almost see him then—the real him. He was in there! I knew that for sure, now. Blake was flung back into the shadows. So was Dean.

Eric never opened his eyes, but his pulse had been weak.

That's why she hates me, I think. Both of us have the same speculation.

He's dead.

Neither of us is sure of it though. Alice and the others were pulling us away before we could confirm.

Before we could take him with us.

He's dead weight, Gemma had said through our heads.

Deadweight? Or just *Dead*?

I try to push the thought out of my head. Soldiers were coming in from all directions. We couldn't take on all of them.

"None of them fired a round at us. Don't you think that's strange?"

Leaves are crunching under Misty's feet. Both her voice and Alice's are low. "Blake needs us alive. It's not a surprise. That's why I tried to grab for the gun. He wouldn't risk shooting me."

You got shot *anyway*, I think.

"You got grazed," Misty continues. "Eric took most of the blow."

"We can't go back. Not for either of them."

The air hitches and a warm breeze piles in to keep us warm.

"They won't like to hear that."

"That's why we can't tell them."

Alice speaks as if she knows both of them are okay. That Eric didn't actually die.

How would she know for sure, though? I didn't see her looking at him when we ran away.

"What should we tell them?"

Anything but . . .

"Nothing. Let them hope for now. I don't think Wanda can handle any more defeat today."

I peek my eyes open to look at her across from me. Her back is to us, curled into a ball.

I'll protect you, I think. I failed when we were kids. I failed when we were on base. But not here. Dean fought so hard to find you . . . and I'd already given up.

Not anymore. She can hate me for the rest of my life, but I wouldn't be able to live with myself if something bad happened to her again.

Never again.

Never again.

The first time I heard this story, it was from Wanda. It was dark, depressing, and overall heart-wrecking. Not trying to pull away from her story but . . . whatever happened to the love of her life, she, nor anyone else, can confirm. I know she refuses to believe he's gone-gone, but I can also read her eyes and see the acceptance of a grieving love.

From "My Thoughts"--SRP

I see what she sees. I feel what she feels. Everything that she is or was or going to be I can understand. It's like she lives through me, but neither of us knows of each other. And yet, all the pain she feels, I feel as my own.

Her thoughts run into mine, sucking me into the world more and more.

I start to become her.

Be her.

I am her.

I am me?

Today was supposed to be the first day back for senior year, but I'll be late. Five weeks late that is.

I've been on this ship for five weeks-almost six by

tomorrow. Locked in a vacuum sealed room, on a ship, in the middle of space. . . Combined that time with a lack of sleep and I've been thrown into a loop.

The darkness drags into eternity.

I knew sleep wasn't coming to rescue me tonight. My cracking limbs, stiff on the floor, are sign enough. It's constantly freezing down here on the bottom level of the ship. It's the only place that's like this. The only room.

She says I'm held here because I won't "cause problems."

I grunt, stiffening my body more. I can't close my eyes long enough to catch some z's. My body aches for warmth.

I clutch the thin blanket around me tighter. It's the only thing that keeps me breathing when I lay on the metal floor; my pillow, a large ground pipe that lies adjacent to the wall I face. My back is toward the gallery window where my guard stands outside, watching. I face the opposite wall.

I don't want them to see me cry silently like I do most nights.

Tonight is no different, but when I hear her voice muffled outside the glass, I fall deathly quiet. I try to relax as if I'm asleep and shift my chin closer to my chest. There's muffled words between the two of them--my guard and her.

Time carries out only for a moment before the intercom comes to life. That's when I know I'm alone with her. My guard has left the room.

I'm glad there's a barrier between us.

Her voice is solemn, "I would bring her back if I could, you know." I know it's genuine. "I loved her too."

The silence carries. I know she's waiting for me to answer. Hoping for it. She wants me to turn around and face her. Give her a reassuring smile and say it's okay . . . I forgive you.

I don't move a muscle.

"I am so, so . . . sorry. I've wronged you in so many ways and I can't take them back." her sadness slowly poisons my heart. "I was only doing my job. I want--I wish . . . I wish you could understand why I do the things I do. If I hadn't--if you only stopped, then . . . then she wouldn't have . . ."

Died?

The intercom clicks off on her growing sobs. The wound is still fresh. Very, very fresh. My eyes burn from the swelling tears as I finally turn to look out the glass. I don't see her, rather, I spot my guard in the shadows coming back to stand in front of the door.

She's gone.

I thought not having friends at school made me alone, but now . . . I'm definitely, absolutely, irrevocably alone.

About the Author:
Since she was little, she's had a passion to tell a story that everyone will love. She's currently aspiring to become a teacher in English. Helping students and kids of all ages with writing is what she strives to do! Being creative is all she knows and feels it will save kids who are discouraged from writing--just as she felt when she was still learning. But the right teachers can change your view and that's her vision. She hopes to be there for her students and be a beacon of hope for when they move forward, no matter where they go.

Recently graduated with her associates from Ranger College, Currently attending Tarleton University for her Education Certificate and Bachelors in English.
Find the Author:
Instagram
@k_k.smith
@ka.lo_art

ACKNOWLEDGMENTS

As everyone says, thank you for reading all the way to the end!

I want to acknowledge YOU--whoever you are--you are someone to behold! You made it to the end when I never expected that of you. It's not that I didn't think you couldn't get to the end, but rather I expected you were bored with it by the first page and gave up. But! You, reading this right now, I mean it with all that makes me, me, I thank you for all your time! I thank you for your words of encouragement and love throughout this process. YOU mean the world to me. Though I might not know all of you, it comes from a place of love that I recognize you! Not only the growing family but my real one.

My dad said he wouldn't read it until it was done. And now, it is! Here you go, Dad! This is what I made! Did you love it as much as the story I first wrote for you when I was little? Or are you still rooting for your character to come back? LOL! And Mom. I can't tell you how much it touches my heart that you took the time out of your busy days to sit down and actually read my book! I love you for that!

Layla! You have always been my closest friend and no amount of time or words can describe how much you mean to me in my heart. You have made my world count! Thank you for that!

I also want to thank my Aunt Shell and Granny! Aunt Shell, you've inspired me that no dream is too big for me to reach. I've taken that to heart and will always remember how much you influence my day to day life with your loving words! Granny. You are a woman of praise! A woman that strives to stimulate my own love for not only the world but myself! If you make it to the end, I hope I can change the world in your eyes. Even more than you've changed mine. You have incased my heart in a hard shell that can never be broken. From saving me from a broken heart and a broken heart yourself, I've learned how much you really have loved and lost in this world. You stand up prouder than any other person that had a broken heart. You understand more than I will ever know and I can't wait for you to look over me when I'm older. You are my golden star! My guardian angel!

Auntie Lauren, you've been my older sister more than my aunt. You support me and always enlighten me on the life I live. You root for me and no matter how strange it is you praise it as more than I thought. Thank you. Truly. Your spirit alone has saved me from giving up so many times I can't even count anymore. I love you so much!

It's been a bumpy and strange ride for not just you, but for me. I had so much fun writing this story, and I hope you liked it enough to let me tell you this is not the last of Alice and her renegades. This story is the first of much more and I hope you'll stay for the true end. I love this story to my very core, and I can't wait to show it to the world someday soon! This is only the beginning, so strap yourself into the wonderful world of the Delam Series! By the end, you'll be thirsting for more of not only Wanda and her friends, but her new connected family, Alice and her renegades!

Until next time, thanks for reading!